GAME OVER!

JOE AND RUTH KRAKOVSKY

TATE PUBLISHING
AND ENTERPRISES, LLC

Published by Tate Publishing & Enterprises, LLC
127 E. Trade Center Terrace | Mustang, Oklahoma 73064 USA
1.888.361.9473 | www.tatepublishing.com

Tate Publishing is committed to excellence in the publishing industry. The company reflects the philosophy established by the founders, based on Psalm 68:11,
"The Lord gave the word and great was the company of those who published it."

Book design copyright © 2014 by Tate Publishing, LLC. All rights reserved.
Cover design by Carlo nino Suico
Interior design by Jomel Pepito

Published in the United States of America
ISBN: 978-1-63122-864-3
Fiction / Action & Adventure
14.04.29

Chapter One

Moving stealthily down the dark, dank passageway leading deeper into the beast's lair feels like walking down the throat of the hungry monster itself. With each nervous step we take, it is slowly swallowing us whole. Who knows what challenges still lay ahead, or if any of us will get out of this alive? We have already lost three good fighters from our group: one to a trap and two others who were defeated in a battle with the dragon guarding the entrance to the tunnel that we are now cautiously making our way through. One wrong move could put us all in danger and our bones would lie here forever, slowly decaying over the centuries, undiscovered by any except perhaps the hungry rats and trolls.

I quickly check on my companions. This is no time to be lax; we must all be on guard. Each needs to be alert and ready to do what they do best.

I am Mandor, man-at-arms, the unofficial leader of this peculiar little band. Following directly behind me is Ragon, the Hooded Ranger. No one really knows what

Joe & Ruth Krakovsky

he looks like as his brown, deer skin cloak covers him from shoulder to knee, and his hood sits so far forward on his head that his face is forever in shadow. One of his few remaining precious arrows is notched in his bow, ready to deliver the sting of death from a distance.

Behind Ragon is Moonbeam, the Fairy Princess of Matterhorn. There is a look of determination in her eyes, turning them from a soft, sky blue to an icy, cold frost. Her long golden curls frame her pale, delicate face and her mouth is always turned slightly up at the corners as if she holds a secret no one else knows. She carries nothing more menacing than a Dogwood twig, but then, the fairy princess is not a fighter. Her value to the group is what lies nestled within the leather pouch fastened securely around her neck by a braided thong. More than once she has proven her worth on this quest by her skillful use of white magic.

Bringing up the rear is Slayer, another man-at-arms like me. You can't have too many heavily armed and armored companions in a place like this. He is larger and more muscular than I but when it comes to brains, I believe that is where my strength exceeds his and where the crack in his strength is revealed.

Just ahead and leading the way is Badger, the thief. He has long, black greasy hair and shifty dark eyes; a face not to be trusted. But trust him we must. Armed with only a long, sharply honed dagger, he uses his dexterity, stealth, and cunning to uncover and avoid the dangers and pitfalls confronting us along the way.

He has stopped in midstride, raising his arm as a signal for us to be still. Although it is very dark, our

6

eyes have adjusted to the gloom so that we all freeze in our tracks. We don't know why he has stopped, or what he sees, but we have to rely on his judgment. Each of us has our strengths and our weaknesses, but together we are strong. Our willingness to work together is the only reason we have made it this far. The darkness swallows him up as he creeps silently ahead to investigate.

Ah, he is returning. We all breathe a sigh of relief as he comes back into view.

"There was a trap up ahead," Badger informs us in a low voice, "but I have rendered it safe and marked it with a circle of five stones. Just a short way past that, the tunnel opens up into a large cavern. On the far side lies an iron gate which is open. That is the good news. The bad news is that it is guarded by a squad of trolls."

"We can take them," boasts Slayer with more confidence than he is probably feeling.

As usual, Ragon just nods without speaking.

Moonbeam doesn't respond to the announcement. I didn't expect that she would. How can she agree to a violence that she doesn't believe in, especially when the only part she will play in it is to try and get us out of any mess we manage to get ourselves into?

I can sense that Badger wants to spring into immediate action, but only because logically, that is the quickest way to finish our quest. We will have to keep an eye on him lest he becomes careless in his rush to reach the treasure. Before we can claim the prize, we have to get through the obstacles; and to get through the obstacles takes time, patience, and skill. And patience does not seem to be one of Badger's strong points.

They are all looking to me, their leader by common consent, to make the final decision.

"Alright then, here's what we will do. Moonbeam, do you have anything in your pouch that can aid us in getting closer to the gate? If you do, then maybe we can be upon them before they have time to close it and sound the alarm."

She wraps her delicate fingers around the little bag of secrets and nods her head. "I think I may have something that will do the trick; whenever you are ready."

"Let's do this," says Slayer, speaking for all of us, as he flexes his bulging muscles under his armor plate causing it to expand and contract as easily as if it was made from the skin of an animal.

The fairy princess reaches into her pouch and pulls out a small, blue glass vial. Pouring a few drops onto her palm, she holds up her open hand and blows softly across it. A mist begins to form, growing larger and denser until it appears to touch the low stone ceiling and the damp sides of the passageway. "Quickly, all of you step inside the protective fog and stay there until you get close to the gate. It won't last long so you must hurry."

By luck or by design, the air current carries the vaporous mass forward. We shuffle within it, keeping as close together as possible so as to all stay concealed within the dark cloud. Finally we can see the trolls, but it appears that they cannot see us approaching them.

Out of the corner of my eye I see Moonbeam following closely behind me. What on earth is she doing here? She is going to get herself killed! She should have stayed back in the tunnel where it was safe. Now I am so aware of her presence it is distracting. How can I put one hundred per cent into the anticipated upcoming battle when I have to worry about her whereabouts and safety? Oh well, it is too late to do anything about it now. We are almost upon them and our protective fog is starting to dissipate.

The visor on my helmet is still raised. Sometimes I prefer it that way because it allows for better vision, especially in dark places. Of course, that also means a loss of protection in the all-important facial area. I do have my rakish good looks to consider, but in this instance I choose to leave it open.

Slayer is the first to strike. Bringing his two-handed sword down on the head of the nearest troll, he splits its ugly skull wide open like a pumpkin, spilling the creature's meager store of slimy gray matter onto the floor.

Before Slayer can pull his blade free of the soggy mass of flesh and bone, Badger moves in. He knows his mission; get to the gate and make sure it remains open. Like a rabbit nimbly weaving its way through the maze of a briar patch, Badger quickly dodges around the surprised trolls, relying on his speed and dexterity to avoid their clumsy attempts to strike him down. Being the dull witted, muscle bound oafs that they are, with most of their strength in their long gorilla-like arms, their power is in the strength of the blows they deliver. Fortunately for us, they are not built for speed.

Ragon lets fly one of his arrows. Without even looking, I know it strikes home. I can hear the roar of rage and pain coming from his intended victim. He will need to retrieve that arrow later. His queue of arrows is running low and we may need them in the future. I just hope that this time he can extract it from the creature's hide without breaking it.

With his arrow launched, Ragon draws his sword and moves forward to assist Badger. They must keep that gate open!

Letting loose with a wild yell, I charge to the right flank. With Slayer on the left, this allows Ragon and Badger to focus on the middle. This play has worked for us a couple of times so far. As a matter of fact, each time we use it we have gotten better at it.

The troll that jumps in front of me is an ugly cuss up close. He squints his yellowish, bloodshot eyes and bares his massive fangs as he prepares to strike me with his club. But I am faster and a swipe of my blade makes him just a bit uglier as I slice off his piggish snout. He squeals and drops his weapon as he attempts to staunch the flood of greenish pus that passes for troll blood. No time or need to finish him off. There are still others to contend with.

Slayer has already dispatched another brute and is swinging his massive sword wildly at the next one. I am concerned that he might be getting a little sloppy and careless, striking out time after time without any real thought. He may be getting caught up in the moment of swordplay rather than remembering that the quest is the reason for the fight. That will surely get him killed one of these times.

As I rush forward to engage another beast, I catch sight of Badger and Ragon working their way closer to the gate. A maddened troll is flailing about, gushing green gunk out of the stumps that once had arms attached to them. At times there is a certain sick humor to Ragon's work.

Curses! Now I have two trolls on me at the same time! Engaging one at a time is easy; two is much more dangerous. I barely have time to strike at the first one when I see the second one trying to get around me. I know he has his sights set on the unprotected Moonbeam. I have to keep him from reaching her before I can finish off the first attacker. I land a lucky hit which at least slows him down somewhat. I have not managed to stop either one yet but at least I know they are both wounded.

Unlike Slayer with his two-handed sword, I carry a one-handed sword along with a shield which I now have to rely on as I deal with these two. My concern for Moonbeam is distracting me. I wish she would have just stayed back. I have to concentrate, find an opening, then strike!

I can't believe it. Here comes a third troll out for blood. I am taking too long. Slayer, not having to worry about protecting a non-fighter, is still working his way forward. A dangerous gap in our line is forming. *Oh no, I'm in trouble; we're in trouble!*

What in the world is she doing? Moonbeam is moving off to the right instead of staying safely behind me. She is trying to draw the attention of my third attacker, challenging him by waving her Dogwood twig as if it is some kind of weapon. I've got to save her!

Throwing all caution aside, I hurl my shield at the troll to my left, mainly in an attempt to draw his attention elsewhere. Using my sword with both hands, I chop down at the one on my right. He tries to block my sword with his club but my razor sharp blade slices right through it. As I turn to engage the lumbering oaf approaching Moonbeam, I blindly swing again at the brute whose club I just ruined. Luck is with me and he clutches at the gaping wound in his throat.

Moonbeam has been backed into a corner. The look of strength and determination in her eyes is her only defense. The misshapen troll is grunting and grimacing as he stalks her and pokes at her with his club. He appears to be amused by her tenacity. Perhaps that is what has kept him from finishing her off already.

"Hey you! Pig face!" I yell, and as he turns to my voice, I lunge forward and thrust my blade deep into his side. He squeals and falls heavily to the ground. After a couple of spasms which jerk his whole body uncontrollably, he finally lies motionless. I have saved her.

"Mandor, behind you!" Moonbeam cries out frantically.

I swivel around and instinctively raise my now shield-less left arm as the troll's wicked blade slashes at an angle across it. Had it not been for my plate armor, he would have managed to render my arm useless. As it is, his blade skims across my armored appendage and heads right for the place where my visor should have been. The tip of his blade slices across my unprotected face. I know that I have made a grave mistake in not wearing my visor and I have possibly lost an eye or at best, I will be sporting a pretty significant scar. That will most certainly cost me.

I try to retrieve my sword, but the blade is too deeply embedded in the dead creature's side, so I have no other choice but to release the hilt which causes me to stumble backwards as he swings again. I have to finish this or I am done for. With a flick of my fingers I slam my visor down just as I launch myself into him. Being so close, he is unable to use his sword against me, so he tries biting my face through my visor. He freezes in stunned surprise as I bury my dagger up to the hilt into his fat belly, giving it a vicious twist causing him to let out an agonizing wail and fall away.

"You are hurt," she cries as she rushes to my side. Reaching into her pouch, Moonbeam withdraws a small packet. Removing a pinch of healing powder she exposes my face wound and sprinkles the magic dust generously into the jagged open gash in an attempt to counteract the poison that had been painted onto the troll's sword tip. Her quick thinking allows me to keep on going.

As I regain possession of my sword and shield, I take stock of our situation. Thanks to Slayer and Ragon, who have finished off the remaining guards, the skirmish is over, the gate is captured, and we are victorious.

Badger approaches us to report. "The way to the treasure is open. I suggest we move quickly before any other inhabitants are alerted to our presence." As he says this his hooded eyes never look directly at me. I guess thieves are supposed to have shifty eyes and be shady looking characters. I have no choice but to take his report as his word. After all, he has not failed us so far.

"Well, what are we waiting for?" asks Slayer. It is obvious this man is anxious to get back into action.

Ragon does not speak. He shows his agreement by yanking out the arrow that had been stuck deeply in the throat of a lifeless troll. I think he intentionally tries to cause that sickening sucking sound generated by breaking the suction as he pulls the arrow free of muscle, fat, and thick skin.

With all in agreement, we prepare to move on.

"I don't like the look of this, Mandor," Moonbeam whispers coming up beside me.

This surprises me as she usually leaves things of a martial matter to us fighting men.

"This is too easy," she says with a worried frown. "And besides, I have a bad feeling about Badger," she whispers in my ear. "I don't trust him."

"We can't worry about him, Moonbeam. This far into it we have no other option but to stick together. That is the only way we can survive. None of us has the ability to make it on our own."

As we enter the large cavern all eyes are at once drawn to a dark blue sapphire the size of a man's fist, sparkling and glowing warmly with a light of its own and resting upon a pagan alter. It is ours for the taking.

Then we hear it. A long, low hissing sound that fills the air. Looking all around, I can't tell where it is originating from.

"Look out!" yells Ragon, as he shoves both Moonbeam and me back towards the gate.

From above our heads drops a creature that lands with an earth shaking thud right on the spot where we had been standing. He must be quite heavy, for his landing has raised a cloud of dust which rolls forth like a wave. Kreator, the cave dweller and protector of the god's jewels, stands upon its two hind legs resembling a bear protecting its cub. He stands at twice the size of any human being and his massive rear claws appear to be the perfect weapon for gutting out the belly of a foe. Its front limbs have claws too, but these look more like the talons of a giant eagle. They would be ideal for grasping and tearing its prey apart piece by piece. The bulky body is completely covered in some type of scale armor. Its neck, long and thick, supports a head, which to me resembles that of a crocodile. Rows of razor sharp teeth, like those of a shark, click and grind as the creatures mouth opens wide and snaps shut over and over again. I don't think his sole intention is to protect the gem from falling into our hands; I believe he is also looking for a meal.

Raising my sword, I immediately charge forward behind my shield. I am the first to strike, but my blade bounces off of the scale armor with a clang, like metal against metal.

Slayer moves in to assist me. We need to try to keep this monster between us until we can discover its weakness. And hopefully it does have a weakness.

Behind us Ragon stands with an arrow notched and ready, but at a loss as to where to send it. If my sword is unable to penetrate that hide then surely an arrow will be even less effective.

Moonbeam is behind us and I am hoping that she has the sense to keep back out of danger's way this time. We are going to have our hands full with this one and I don't need anything additional to worry about.

I see Badger is hugging the wall, sliding along it inch by slow inch. He seems to be trying to sneak undetected around behind the beast.

Slayer strikes out again and I follow suit. Our swords don't seem to be of any use against Kreator's protected hide. The strikes aren't fazing him one bit and all we are doing is raising a spray of sparks with each hit.

I draw a little too close and the beast lashes out at me with its long sharp talons. They cut right through my shield as well as the plate covering my left arm. I sustain only a minor wound, but my shield is destroyed so I cast the useless item aside.

On and on we fight, slashing and dodging, striking and ducking; three warriors against this seemingly undefeatable giant. But where the heck is Badger?

Kreator has taken notice of Moonbeam, the Fairy Princess of Matterhorn, and is beginning to work his way toward her. I stay directly in front of him in an effort to use my body as a barrier between the two. Slayer manages to get in a strike to Kreator's thick neck but he fails to inflict any damage. This causes the creature to pause and snap his teeth at Slayer in protest, so it is at this moment that Ragon lets his arrow fly. The projectile strikes home, burying deeply into the beast's left eye. It lets out a terrifying hiss and is flailing its head from side to side, trying to dislodge the foreign object causing him so much pain.

Immediately I strike again, trying for its throat this time. Maybe there is a vulnerable area there. No luck. I have only managed to make him angrier than ever.

He turns his attention back to me, spitting forth a fireball which strikes me square in the chest. The impact knocks me off my feet, and as I land hard on my back I realize that I must quickly shed my armor, for I can see the glow and hear the sizzle from the flaming spittle that is eating its way through my protective covering.

Ragon and Slayer are continuing to distract the monster so I raise myself up and start to pull off as much of my armor as I can. But it is no use. I know that I am done for.

I look over at Moonbeam and realize that she is down. From the smoke rising from her chest I know that she too was hit. It wasn't much, compared to what struck me, but she is a delicate creature and wears no protective cover.

I crawl over to her and I can see that she is dying. I quickly fumble around in her pouch for her healing packet. Yanking it free from the bag, I yell, "Save us!"

Shakily she pulls out a sticky paste wrapped in a leaf. "Swallow this," she croaks weakly.

"Here, you take some too," I beg.

"No, Mandor, there is not enough for two. To make you strong enough to continue, you must take it all. You will have to finish this quest without me."

I know she is right but that doesn't make it any easier. I am very aware that in order to save myself, I am killing her. She is looking very pale and so weak and vulnerable. I reach out and touch my fingertips to her cheek in farewell and with great reluctance I put the paste into my mouth. "I will be victorious, Moonbeam. For you! I promise."

She smiles gently in reply.

I see what is left of my fine blade is slowly dissolving away under a wisp of acrid smoke. It hasn't done me any good anyway since it cannot penetrate Kreator's armored skin. I see the still bodies of Ragon and Slayer lying twisted in the dirt and my heart skips a beat to realize that they are dead and all of the beast's attention is now focused on me.

Glancing over I see the dying figure of Moonbeam. It really is a shame about her. Sure, the quest is what is important, but I have grown extremely fond of her. She looks over at Kreator and then at what is left of my sword. Without a word and using the last bit of her strength she holds up her Dogwood twig. I accept it with genuine gratitude, for it is all she has left to give. With that she closes her beautiful eyes for the last time.

I see that Badger has made it around past the creature and is skulking in the shadows behind him. Even as I watch, he races over to the altar and snatches up the jewel, unnoticed by Kreator since his attention is solely on me. Without so much as a backward glance the backstabbing thief dashes off back the way we came, leaving me to my certain doom.

Kreator is toying with me now, probably since he doesn't see me as much of a threat now that he has disposed of everyone else. He is advancing toward me slowly, confident that he has won. The twig in my hand is my last defense. It is just a thin piece of crooked wood with a few small buds, one of which has sprouted into a tiny leaf; Moonbeam's final gift to me. She looks so peaceful laying there. I have heard that this creature has a particular taste for fairies. The thought of him devouring something so pure and lovely fills me with determination and rage.

Ah, I can feel her potion starting to rejuvenate me. Power and strength are surging through me and I spring to my feet yelling in defiance, "This is for Moonbeam!" as I leap up and jam the Dogwood twig into his remaining good eye.

A terrific screech pierces the air as Kreator thrashes his head wildly while trying to blindly grasp the twig with his talons. I can only watch in fascination as his protective scales begin to flake off, uncovering the underlying tissue which is liquefying and dripping down his body; forming puddles of bloody goo on the ground all around him. The beast is not just dying; it is dissolving, or melting, like some giant molten candle. Then it becomes clear to me. That one tiny leaf, freshly sprouted from a bud, must be the most toxic substance on earth to the mighty creature known as Kreator. And she must have known that all along, my Fairy Princess of Matterhorn.

"GAME OVER!"

The words flash across the screen in large, bold letters.

Man, this has got to be the coolest game ever! I have played just about every computer-based, fantasy role playing game out there, but none have come close to this one. It is so realistic.

I have heard stories from some of the older people about the old role playing fantasy games that they use to play back in the seventies and eighties, way back before computer games were invented and before I was even born. They fondly reminisce about a group of friends spending an entire evening sitting around a table, keeping track of their character's movements on graph paper as they created a map of the dungeon they were exploring. They had to rely on someone to describe what their characters were doing and seeing, and they would fight their pretend battles with little painted lead figures where the outcome was determined by a roll of the various multisided dice.

Hah! How lame can you get? I would have died of boredom! I can't imagine anything better than standing in front of my flat screen TV and entering a virtual world where I am in control of my fate; a fantasy world that I can enter into, and where I can interact with people from anywhere in the world. And all the while I can experience firsthand what my character is seeing and doing thanks to the latest high tech computers and games.

The only thing I didn't like about this particular game is the outcome. Sure, I survived, but so did Badger, that traitor! Moonbeam was right about him. It's kind of sad that she had to die, whoever she was. I guess I'll never know who the real person behind that character was. She was just a faceless voice in the headset who brought her character to life on the screen.

Oh boy, the points are being calculated. I wonder what I got. Will it be enough to stay in the running?

> Moonbeam-KIA...Slayer-KIA...Ragon-KIA...Badger-100 gold pieces...Mandor-500 gold pieces.

What? I can't believe it. Why should Badger get anything? He left me there to be slaughtered and ran off with the treasure...Wait, there is a ruling coming up on the screen.

> Badger did not follow the instructions as stated for this quest. He abandoned his team and did not remain to assist in slaying Kreator; therefore his gold is forfeit and has been awarded to Mandor.

Wow! I bet that guy is fuming. It serves him right though. Oh well, I'm happy with what I got. I am not only in first place, but I have accumulated the highest score of any man-at-arms in this whole competition! I can't wait to tell Mark. And I can't wait until...

"Jeb Stuart Maxwell! Did you finish your homework and clean your room?"

"Aw, geez Mom, I'm working on it!"

Chapter Two

Standing at the bus stop waiting for the school bus to arrive, I can hardly wait for my best buddy Mark to get here. I am excited to tell him about this latest game. He loves video games as much as I do. In fact that is how we became best friends to begin with.

Mark has lived here in California all of his life but because my dad is in the military, we have moved around a lot. It wasn't until I was in the fifth grade, when he was promoted to the rank of colonel, that we moved here. And it wasn't easy coming into this particular school in the middle of the year. The kids here weren't very welcoming so I was pretty much a loner for the first month or so until one day at recess when I pulled out my handheld video game system and started playing to occupy my time. This curly-haired kid came over next to me to watch me play. He made some suggestions and gave me some pointers on how to beat that particular game and from that day we became fast friends.

He and I are pretty similar in the things we like to do but our personalities differ in that I am more serious while he is more likely to see the humor in things. He has these cat-like green eyes that always have a twinkle in them like he about to burst out laughing at any second. We both have brown hair but where his is curly, mine is stick straight, and he keeps his short while I wear mine long enough to get in my eyes if I don't keep pushing it back.

We are both considered short by high school freshman standards with me standing at five foot two and him only about an inch taller. My mom says I still have plenty of time to grow and I have to say that I sure hope she is right. But then she is biased and thinks I am the handsomest kid around. She tells me that with my big, brown eyes and unusually long eyelashes, the girls will be going crazy over me. Well Mom; I am still waiting for *that* to happen.

"Hey Stuart!" Mark yells, while still a half block away. "How was that game?"

He is as anxious to hear about it as I am to tell him so I quickly fill him in on the details of the game and all of the characters' adventures.

"Oh man, Stuart, it sounds really cool. I wish I could have been there but when my mom found out how much homework I had to do, she wouldn't let me go out."

"I wish you could have been there too, Mark. You would have loved it. The graphics were awesome. Like 3D! You just push a button and flick your wrist and your character draws his weapon and uses it any way you want it to. Heck, you could make him juggle swords if you felt like it. And the characters are so cool. They even show emotion according to what is happening at the time. They react like people would in real life, like laughing, scowling, and even crying. You make your avatar speak by using a headset and it actually moves its mouth and uses facial expressions. You can also interact with the other characters in your game. It was awesome!"

"Yeah, it sounds like it. That game sure sounds better than the crummy one I've been playing. The newer version is way better, but my parents refuse to buy it for me. They ask me what the difference is and then when I tell them, they just shake their heads and tell me what a waste of money it is and about how it was when they were young, and how they didn't need to upgrade everything they owned. They made do with what they had and were thankful for it. They don't understand that times have changed from when they were young. But that's alright. My birthday is coming up so I'll just ask my grandma for it."

"I know what you mean about times being different, Mark. My mom told me about this one game she used to play, I forget the name; you know the one that looks like you're playing air hockey on the screen with two little sticks and a ball? Even now she says she would like to play that one again."

Mark laughs. "Yeah, I know the one you mean. It was called 'Bong' or something like that."

My mom and dad were married for almost twenty years before they finally had me so they are older than some of the other kids' parents. Back when they were kids nobody had a computer. I don't even know if they were invented yet. It makes me wonder what guys like Mark and I would have done for entertainment if we had been born back in those days, before they discovered fire, and computer games and stuff.

"So do you have any idea what game you will be playing next?" he asks.

"No, that's one thing that makes it so interesting. I never know what is in store for me from one level to the next. You see, in the competition I am a renegade mercenary who is recruited by this Being, whoever he is, to travel through time and space, in order to carry out different missions for him. I am presented with a scenario, a character, and given certain tasks to accomplish, but how I choose to carry them out is up to me."

"That sounds really cool, Stuart. I wish I could try it."

I can tell he is hoping for me to invite him to play and I feel bad that I can't. "I'm really sorry, but the contestants have already been chosen and they aren't accepting any new ones."

"That's okay. Maybe I can watch you play sometime."

"That would be great, Mark. I'll have to let you know when I will be playing though. This isn't like your usual game where you can turn it on whenever you want to and can replay as many times as necessary to win. This is more like some outside entity is controlling the game, so there is constant communication, but it is only one way. They let me know by e-mail when the game will take place and I don't find out until then what the game is or how much time is allotted to finish it. It's like whoever the controller is, this 'game god,' can make each situation different for different people. At least that is what I kind of figured out for myself by reading the blogs. Besides that, there are other contestants who log in and join you on some of your missions. You might be on a quest with a certain character and after it is over you might not see them again until two or three games later, if at all. It all depends on whether they survive that long, because once you are dead, you are out of the game for good. If you survive, you are awarded pieces of gold according to how well you did. The more gold you accumulate, the more points you have, but points can also be deducted for any injuries you sustain. Another thing that sets this game apart is that you cannot use your virtual gold to buy better weapons or extra lives, nor are you awarded special abilities as you advance. It is more like real life in that your character's skills and abilities increase as you learn to master each game."

He shrugs his shoulders and looks puzzled, "So what is the point in getting the gold pieces if you can't buy better weapons or more lives?"

"I haven't figured that out yet," I admit. "Maybe it's a way of accumulating more points. You are expected to survive the whole game with whatever is given to you at the beginning of that particular game. That is what makes it so challenging. Plus the whole thing is timed so you have to successfully complete the assigned quest before the time runs out or you are done for good."

"How did you hear about this competition?" he asks curiously.

"I accidently came across it when I was surfing the internet. It was on an obscure website that looked like it was intentionally hidden so that only really serious gamers would be able to find it. I saw it mentioned in a blog, which led to another site, which led me to another and after quite a bit of searching, I finally found it."

"You lucky dog," Mark responds good-naturedly. "Well anyway, I'm glad that Badger guy lost his gold for being such a jerk. It's too bad about that Moonbeam girl though."

"Yeah," I agree, "I kind of liked her. She was pretty decent."

Mark smirks and raises one eyebrow. "So, you liked her, huh? Just what kind of 'interacting' were you doing with her?" Even though he can tell from my expression that his teasing is making me uncomfortable he adds jokingly, "Oh, that's right, I forgot, you already have a girlfriend."

I know he is referring to Becki. He knows that Becki Everest isn't my girlfriend, and he also knows that I secretly really like her a lot, but he is just goofing around so I decide to just let his remarks go. I laugh and punch him playfully in the arm. "Mark, my friend, you can be such a jerk."

He laughs too and we break off our conversation as the yellow bus rumbles into view. I look around at the other kids as I begin to board. I quickly scan the mass of faces as I search for a seat, but the one that I am hoping to see isn't among them. I wonder where Becki is today.

Chapter Three

"Is your homework finished, Stuart?"

"It's done, Mom!"

"Don't mouth off to your Mother."

"Dad, I'm not!"

"Did you clean your room like I asked?"

"Yes, ma'am."

"You did? Then why are there dirty clothes still scattered all over your room? How am I supposed to do the laundry if your dirty clothes are not where they are supposed to be?"

A deeper voice rumbles up the stairs. "Do we need to ground you?"

"No, sir!" I know what that means: no computer games. To be grounded right now when I am waiting to be notified about my next mission would be the worst. If I accept the challenge and then don't show up for it because I'm grounded my character would be considered dead and I would be out of the game for good. If that happens then Mom and Dad might as well kill the real me too!

"Dinner is ready, dear. You can finish your room later."

"Yes, ma'am." Whew. Saved by the... *Oh darn, it's meatloaf.* I don't care much for the taste of meatloaf. I don't even like the way it smells, but I sure don't want to cause a scene now. Whatever I do, I have to make sure not to give Dad any reason to talk about grounding me, because if he does, I'm done for. I can usually talk my mom into and out of things, especially if I say that I am sorry and will never do it again, and give her a hug. But with my dad, his word is law, as if by showing no mercy will somehow make me a better man someday. I guess he's been in the army for too long. If he were to ground me, there would be no amount of persuasion that I could give him to make him change his mind. All of my research and practice to get to the level that I am right now would have been for nothing. So I just keep my opinion of the menu to myself and eat, nod, and smile.

Mom starts off the dinner conversation with, "I heard a couple of women today in the supermarket talking about the Everest family. They were saying that it looks like they will be losing their house. The bank foreclosed on it and now they have to get out. That poor family!"

Everest? That's Becki's family! So maybe that is why she wasn't at the bus stop today. I try to look like the only thing on my mind is stuffing my face with food, but Mom has my full attention as she continues.

"I knew Martin Everest had been laid off from his job with that computer game company, and he lost all of his stock options when the company folded, but I never thought it would come to them losing their home. I wonder why they were targeted to lose their house when there are so many other people in the same predicament who are being allowed to stay in their homes indefinitely for free. Why don't they treat everybody the same? What will happen to the poor Everests? Where will they go? How will they live?"

Mom is acting like this is her problem to solve. She really cares about people and she is always volunteering to help others less fortunate than we are. We aren't rich. I guess we are what you would call middle class, but even if we were poor, I think she would still be the same way.

Dad puts down his fork and is clearing his throat. I can tell when he is about to start preaching. Whenever he puts down whatever he is doing and clasps his hands together like he is about to say grace, you can be sure there is a lecture coming.

"I know Martin Everest from the club. We have had some conversations on the golf course so I know he has always tried to stay out of debt. He never bought a car unless he could pay cash for it and the one credit card they had was always paid in full each month. They had less than ten years left until their mortgage was paid off, therefore it would be in the bank's best interest to foreclose on their house. That way the bank can sell it and make a profit, or at least get some of their money back. The sad thing is that a man like Martin Everest always tries to do what is right and he loses his house, while you have other people in debt up to their eyeballs, who can't or won't pay their bills, and they get all of the breaks because they know how to manipulate the system. Where is the justice in that?"

Oh boy, there is no stopping Dad now.

"He probably won't apply for food stamps or any other type of public aid for that matter. He is much too proud even though they are one family that could legitimately use the state aid. There are so many other people out there who are just taking advantage of public aid programs, who should be cut off, but aren't. Some families truly need this help, but there are others who think of it as free money. My buddy was in the grocery store the other day and there was a woman with a whole cart full of food, like steaks, pork chops, and ham, which we can barely afford ourselves. She opened a wallet full of money only to pull out her food stamp card to pay. Another time someone even offered to pay for his groceries with their card if he gave her his cash. Can you believe that?"

When he starts talking politics, Dad can really go off on a tangent. Although he does make some good points occasionally, I can do without hearing his rants, especially over dinner.

I can tell Mom is about to speak again. The little frown lines on her forehead have deepened and she is looking intently at her plate as if her meatloaf is the most interesting thing she has ever seen, when really I know she is thinking hard about what she is going to say. She and I have a pretty close relationship so we can usually read each other's body language fairly well.

I was right. She looks up and says, "Those women also said that they have had to sell most of their furniture and household items already, but much of it went at a fraction of the original cost. It's a shame the way some people take advantage of others when they fall on hard times. I feel so badly for them, especially the poor children."

Dad takes a bite of potatoes and adds, "You would think that a man like Martin would have been able to find a job by now. With his education and talent, he should be able to find something. The military is always looking for good men and women with brains and leadership qualities."

If it were up to my Dad, he would make every guy who could not find a job join the armed forces whether they wanted to or not. When he believes in something, it is hard to get him to change his mind. Mom has beliefs too but she doesn't try to push them on people. She has the ability to see everyone's side and she doesn't judge them. She has such a big heart. How did my Dad ever end up with someone like her? He sounds like he doesn't have any sympathy for the Everests at all. At least Mom is trying to be fair.

"Now Bill, I'm sure he has been looking," she says calmly. "But the jobs are just not out there right now. Nobody is hiring."

Mom would take them in and everyone else too, if she could, like a shelter takes in abandoned puppies. And she is probably right about Mr. Everest just not being able to find a job. There might be serious money to be made in the gaming industry, but it is a real cutthroat business right now. I know this from the articles I read and the blogs that I follow religiously.

Oh man, here goes Dad again.

"Well, if it were me, I would not be holding out for the managerial position, or the six figure job. I would take whatever I could find to make sure that my family had food on the table and a place to sleep!"

Dad would probably want to drown those abandoned puppies.

"Oh Bill, I am sure that Martin is doing everything he can to provide for his family."

Dad interrupts her with, "He should be trying harder! Instead, he sends his wife out to work like a slave while he hangs out in coffee shops drinking lattes, or whatever other girly drink they serve, while he spends the day there surfing the internet. He should be out looking for work."

Man, Dad can be so judgmental! It is true that Mrs. Everest works long hours opening Gas Mart and closing Burger Haven. I know this because rumors in school are saying that Becki had to give up her after school activities just so she could be at home to watch her younger brother while her mom is working. If Dad wasn't so old fashioned he would know that the internet is the most efficient way to find and apply for jobs these days.

There! I'm done eating. "May I be excused?"

"Yes," Dad grumbles. "Now go clean your room like your mother said."

"Yes, sir."

I trudge up the stairs and stand in the doorway looking around my bedroom. I don't even know where to begin in here. I guess Mom is right; my room is kind of a mess. The thing is, I like it this way and I actually know where everything is right now.

It is kind of ironic for my dad to order me to clean my room when Mom is always after him to clean up his desk. He uses the same argument with her that I do, saying he knows where everything is when it is messy; but I am not allowed to use that excuse. His desk is one of those cool, old roll tops where you have to slide the cover up to expose the desk underneath, along with all these little cubby holes where you can stash different stuff. Only she makes him keep it closed, especially when we have company, because it is so cluttered with folders and papers that he has absolutely no room whatsoever to even use the desktop for writing on.

I am not very good at organizing so it is hard to know where I should start. I guess the easiest thing would be to gather my laundry. I pick up a shirt lying over the back of my desk chair. I was going to wear it to school tomorrow because it is one of my favorites. Well maybe not, because it smells funny, even to me. I'm not even going to smell those socks sticking out from under the bed; they are going straight into the dirty pile. I am kind of curious though. I wonder just how bad they do smell. *Auk! Why did I do that?* They smell even worse than Mom's meatloaf!

Okay, I think I got everything; now to take them down to the laundry room.

Like a man carrying a heavy burden, I make my way down to the washing machine, dropping the occasional article of clothing and grumbling impatiently when bending down to retrieve it. It wouldn't do to let Mom think this was too easy of a job. I plop the clothes into the already overflowing clothes basket for Mom to sort out later. Just like Dad, I can't figure out what colors or materials go together for a load. I guess he and I do have some things in common. It's just too bad they are all faults.

On my way back to my bedroom I glance into the computer room. No one is in there. Maybe I should take a quick break and check to see if I have any emails.

I sit down and start poking away at the keys. Mom calls it chicken pecking because I only use my two index fingers to type with. I repeat to myself the familiar questions and answers as I give the correct responses. Finally, the website. Login: 49215. Password: bEcki109.

It's a good thing I checked. There is a new mission offered to me; a short one this time, on Thursday night at nine o'clock. Should I take it? If I accept, I will be committed to it. I should get Mom's permission first but I am supposed to be cleaning my room right now. I make the decision and click on the "accept" button. I will worry about getting permission later.

Chapter Four

Oh great! Here it is Thursday afternoon and I still haven't asked about staying up and using the computer and the TV. Mom is always scolding me for putting things off until the last minute but I don't do it on purpose. Time just gets away from me somehow, and before I know it I'm scrambling around trying to do everything in the zero hour. Well, better late than never I guess.

I find my mom in the kitchen putting away groceries. "Hi, Mom."

"Hello, Stuart. How was your day at school?"

"Oh, it was okay. Here, let me help you with these." I grab a box of cereal out of one of the shopping bags and shove it in the cabinet.

"Why thank you, Stuart. That was very thoughtful of you." After a pause she smiles and asks suspiciously, "Is there something you want?"

Doggone it! How does she always know when I want something?

"Well, being as you mentioned it," I begin. "I would like to use the computer for a game tonight. It is a little bit later than usual, but they say that it is only a short game. Do you think I could stay up and play?"

Good, she's still smiling. "How late is late?"

"It starts at nine."

Uh-oh, now she is frowning. "That *is* late. I don't know. This is a school night. Why can't you play earlier?"

"It's a preset time. You either have to play when it's scheduled, or you forfeit your spot. If you accept and then fail to log in you are disqualified, and you aren't allowed to participate in their future challenges."

"So I am assuming that you have already accepted?"

At my guilty nod of affirmation she sighs. "Don't they know that kids have school?"

"Well, yeah, I'm sure they know that, but it is probably because a lot of the players are older. I compete against adults and beat them." It sounded good in my head, but from her deeper frown I think I may have said the wrong thing.

Sounding concerned now she asks, "Just what kind of things do they do in these games?"

"Nothing in particular, Mom; they're just games."

"I think I had better check this game out, Stuart. I suppose you can play, but only if I can be there to see it."

This isn't quite the answer that I wanted to hear, but at least she didn't say no.

———

All evening I have been on my best behavior. My room is clean and my homework is done. There is only fifteen more minutes until game time. "Okay, Mom," I call down the stairs, "I need to log in now."

"I'll be right there, Stuart."

My dad is watching something on the history channel so I'm not able to hook up to the flat screen. The computer monitor will have to do for tonight's game but I am just glad that I get to play at all. I need to log in now so Mom doesn't see my password. I'm sure she would think it is "so cute" that I am using a girl's name and I don't feel like being teased about it in my own home. There's enough of that stuff going on in school.

Good, here she comes, just in time. Now, how can I say this without hurting her feelings? "Okay, Mom, I am going to have to concentrate. These games are fast moving, and I won't have time to explain what all is going on."

"I understand," she says with a feigned sorrowful expression. "You won't have time to explain to your dear, old mother all of the complicated things that she just cannot possibly understand with her simple little mind."

"No, that's not it," I say, afraid that I might have hurt her feelings. Then I see from her sly smile that she is just messing around with me and I smile back and say, "But seriously, it can get pretty intense. The graphics are very realistic. Wait until you see. It looks so real that you might even think it's a DVD. I have to warn you, they sometimes get a little gory."

Greetings Number 49215. Today's mission will require you to be ever alert, and to react quickly and decisively.

Gee, I wonder what they have in store for me?

The Queen of Austria is holding a celebration for her child's first birthday. It is your mission to guard this little one from harm. Should an assassin appear, you must be prepared to deal with them in a manner that will not endanger your young charge nor upset him in any way. As per usual, any weapons and equipment will become available to you once you arrive on site.

This should be interesting. I need to keep my eyes open for an assassin. I wonder how I will recognize them.

Alright, here goes nothing. "Here we go, Mom, it's starting."

What in the world is this? This is unlike any other game I have played. These graphics look like an old fashioned children's video game with cartoon-like characters. There is a chubby baby, wearing nothing but a diaper on his bottom and a crown on his round, little head, sitting in a solid gold highchair on a raised, red velvet platform. The elaborately decorated room is crowded with well-dressed guests, young and old who have come to celebrate the child's birthday. Balloons and streamers are everywhere and gifts are piled high all around the highchair. The queen is greeting her guests as they come through the door, so it is up to me to guard the royal prince.

"Oh, look how adorable he is!" Mom squeals, in the high-pitched voice she uses when speaking to infants.

I don't make any comment about the baby. I need to get right down to business. "I better check to see what weapons and equipment they have issued me… Wait, this can't be right. The only thing listed in my inventory is one of those small wooden paddles with a rubber ball attached to the end of a piece of elastic. That is all I get?"

"Oh no," Mom says now. "The baby is starting to cry. You better do something."

I try to take him out of the highchair but I can't. "I can't pick him up. The game won't let me. I don't know what to do." When it comes to babies, I am at a loss as to what makes them happy.

"Try using your paddle ball," she suggests. "Maybe you can entertain him with that."

Since I have no idea how to take care of a baby, I take her advice and give it a try. Well I'll be; it's working! One minute the kid is bawling puddles of tears and now suddenly he is hiccupping and giggling with joy. I guess it is a good thing Mom is here. She may not know anything about video games but she does know how to handle babies.

"Way to go Mom, thanks! That did the trick. Now keep your eyes open for any suspicious looking…Aw, Mom, please don't do that to my hair while I'm playing my game." Whenever she gets into one of her mushy mom moods she starts running her fingers through my hair and I end up looking like one of those fuzzy-haired troll dolls with their hair sticking up every which way.

A clown with a big red nose, orange hair, and wearing the typical colorful baggy clothes and big, floppy shoes enters the room. I don't like clowns.

"That is one creepy looking clown, Stuart. Maybe you should keep him away from the baby so he doesn't scare him." Either she has played this game before, or her motherly instincts are kicking in.

I try to stop the colorful intruder from getting closer to the birthday boy. "It's not letting me block him and I don't have any weapons!" I have never been this flustered in a game before.

"Use your paddle!" Mom yells excitedly.

But of course! Why didn't I think of that? Taking careful aim so I don't hit any of the guests, I smack the ball in the clown's direction. I hit him in the face once, twice, and finally I hit him directly on his big red nose. There is a loud honk and he rockets around the room deflating like a balloon that has been blown up and let loose before it has been securely tied shut. The royal baby thinks this is hilarious and is cracking up like crazy, and so is Mom.

"Look out, Stuart!" She is pointing to a second clown waddling into view like a drunken penguin.

The party guests keep getting in the way but my aim is better now so I manage to avoid hitting any of them and I pop his nose on the first shot. Again, it lets out a loud honk and deflates comically making the baby laugh harder.

"Watch out, there's another one!" Wow, Mom is really getting into this now.

Honk!

"And another one! Be careful, don't hit that lady!"
Honk!

The creepy clowns are appearing faster now. The baby is giggling hysterically, which makes Mom laugh so hard she snorts. That almost makes me lose control but I stifle the urge to join in with the fun. I have to concentrate.

The fat, little prince is bouncing up and down in his seat squealing with glee when all of a sudden he lets out an obscenely loud fart. I can't help but smile at that one but I continue deflating assassins as fast as I can paddle the ball. So far I have kept them all at bay. Now the baby's face is turning beet red as he squeezes out a mess into his diaper. There is a big, lumpy bulge in it and a yellow puddle is forming around him, and Mom is laughing so hard she is crying.

"Be careful, Mother Dear, if you laugh too hard the same thing might happen to you," I warn. This just makes her laugh all the harder.

Oh my gosh, now the baby is reaching into his diaper and pulling out handfuls of brown glop and starts throwing it at the clowns. He hits one round red nose and takes him out. I can't keep a straight face any longer.

I hear Dad's voice coming from the next room. "What's going on in there?" By the time he walks in, the game is over and I have won.

"Oh Bill, you missed it. Your son is quite the babysitter!" With that she gives me a kiss on the cheek, ruffles my hair one last time, and gets up to leave. "Make sure you brush your teeth before bed."

"Yes, ma'am," I say as she walks out the door. Dad just stands there shaking his head for a moment and then he follows her out. I kind of wish he had joined us in the fun, but realistically I know that would never happen.

I have to wait for them to tally my score. Thanks to Mom, I think I did pretty well.

> Congratulations, number 49215, on a mission well done. The queen is well pleased with your service and has rewarded you with ten gold coins.

Ten coins? That's it? Ten measly coins? That can't be right, unless maybe this was just a training round. Now that I think about it; that is probably what it was. One blog said that if they stick in a training round, it is more for your amusement and practice rather than for any monetary gain. Well it definitely was amusing and I can always use the practice. But hopefully the next game will be more challenging and will be worth more coins.

Chapter Five

It has already been a week since I played the last game. Any day now I should be getting an email explaining how and when to play the next one. I just hope there isn't something anybody wants to watch on TV at the same time. That would stink. If it is between my using it for my game or Dad using it for one of his shows, I know who the winner will be. I will be stuck using the small computer monitor which isn't half as cool looking as the big screen. I have run cables from the computer down to the flat screen so that all I have to do is plug them in and I am all set to go.

I better check my email as soon as I get home. Things would be a heck of a lot easier if I had a decent phone like everybody else. Then I could check my email between classes. But Dad says I don't need one of those fancy gadgets. He thinks that all I would need a phone for is to call home in an emergency. When I try to explain how technology is advancing, and how all the kids have a cell phone that they can also use for texting and the internet and that some even get a new and improved one every year, he just says that is a waste of natural resources, a source of pollution, and is like flushing your money down the toilet. Then he reminds me of how our land line rotary telephone that we inherited from my grandma is over sixty years old and still works just fine. I swear, he is so old fashioned he would have been right at home living with the cavemen.

I have to laugh though whenever I think of the first time Mark used our telephone. Like most kids my age who are growing up with computers, he can figure out enough to work his way around any computer screen, but that first time he picked up the telephone receiver and saw the dial, he was at a loss as to how to make it work. I shouldn't laugh because I would have probably been just as stumped as he was had I not grown up with it.

My dad is so far behind the times that I'm surprised he even gave in and got us our big screen plasma TV. But if our old clunker of a television had not finally broken down I'm sure we would still be using it. Even then, he wanted to bring down the old black and white from the attic until Mom talked him out of it. She said if you have to go through all the trouble of buying adapters and hooking everything up to the satellite and DVD player anyway, you may as well be able to watch a new color screen with a clear picture rather than an old black and white that will probably die soon. Yay Mom, for bringing us out of the dark ages!

I have asked for a new computer several times over the past couple of years with always the same response. The computer we have still works. Are you kidding me? Our system is so old that everything would be out of date by now if I hadn't taught myself to upgrade it myself. Mark gave me his old broken down computer, which I took apart, using some of the parts to update our own. I have become pretty good at figuring out what is wrong with it when there is a problem and I have even gotten rid of several viruses from ours as well as from Mark's.

My dad is always complaining that they don't make things like they use to, which to him is always a bad thing. There is one thing though that I do agree with him about and that is cars. Even I think that today's cars are junk; expensive junk. None of them can compare to Dad's old, rebuilt Mustang. Of course, I could be biased because I put in a lot of sweat helping him refurbish that beauty. You could never do that with a newer model car. The new ones are mostly made from plastic and fiberglass and everything is computerized. If anything goes wrong, you have to either take them to an expert who has the technology, knowhow, and special equipment to work on them or you have to buy a new one.

Dad's car is made of metal. The bumpers are real chrome and boy do they shine! The experts have given Mom's newer car a good safety rating because it is equipped with air bags. The Mustang doesn't have or even need airbags. The body and frame are strong enough where if there is an accident, the car isn't going to crumple up like an accordion like a new one would.

When I get my driver's license I would love to drive that Mustang to school!

Your next game will commence on Friday, the Twelfth of October, at four o'clock. Teams will be assigned at random fifteen minutes before the start of the event.

Another team challenge. I hope I get a good team member. It's too bad that Moonbeam character isn't still around. I wouldn't mind having her as a partner again. I'll just have to make do with whoever they give me. All that matters is that I log in on time. Oh no, there is a thirty dollar entry fee for this one! I don't have that kind of money plus it says you need a credit card and I don't have one of those either.

Hmmm, I wonder where Mom is. Oh good, she is working on her pottery. That usually puts her in a mellow mood. This is a perfect time to ask her.

"Hi, Mom, whatcha doing?" Oh brother! I'm off to a brilliant start. It's obvious what she is doing.

"Hello, Stuart," she laughs. "What do you need?"

How *does* she do that? I guess it's a mom thing to be able to read your kid's mind.

"Oh nothing. I was just wondering if I could have an advance on my allowance?"

"An advance? What on earth for?"

I try to play it cool but it's hard because I really want this. "It's for an entry fee. You know, for that game competition. I made it through that last level, with your help." I glance at her to see if she is pleased that I gave her credit for helping me win but she is still intent on working with her clay. "Now they have set up a new game but this one has an entry fee and I already spent my allowance."

"Now Stuart," she sighs. "We've talked about this before. You need to manage your money better so that you won't get into these situations. Besides, all of your other games were free. It hardly seems fair for them to start asking for money now that you are so far into it. Are you sure this isn't just a scam?"

I'm trying not to freak out now. I have to get this entry fee. "No, Mom. This fee is a one-time thing. I promise this is the only time I will have to pay. After this it will be free for those who are good enough to move on to the final game. And I promise I'll be more careful with my money from now on." I give her my best sad puppy dog look. *Good she saw that.* Although she goes back to concentrating on her work, I think she is at least considering it. "Please Mom?" I plead hopefully.

Finally she looks up at me, and just when I think she is about to give in, she says the dreaded four words that make my heart sink. "Go ask your father."

Arg! That is not what I wanted to hear. He will say no for sure, so I give it one last try. "Come on Mom, please?"

"Go on, go ask your father. I think he is in the garage."

I hang my head and shuffle off with just enough drama to possibly make her feel guilty for turning me away in my time of need. Dad will probably tell me to go out and earn the money myself. But even if I could, I would still need them to let me use their credit card on line. Well, here goes nothing. It's do or die.

Oh good, he is working on his car. Now if only he is in a good mood.

I clear my throat to get his attention. "Um, Dad?"

No answer. And then finally a distracted, "Yes?"

I'm starting to get nervous. What if he says no?

"I was wondering if... Do you think that..."

"What is it, Stuart? Just spit it out."

"Could I have an advance on my allowance I made it to the next level this is the only time that I have to pay I am doing well and you always said—"

"Slow down, tell me what you want and hand me that screwdriver, the left handed one."

Oh good, he is trying to be funny. I'll play along.

"You mean the one with the red handle?" They all have red handles.

That makes him look up. Gotcha!

Now I have his full attention so I 'spit it out.' "What I need is an advance on my allowance to cover the entry fee for the contest I've been competing in. This is the only time I need to pay because I am getting into the final eliminations. I'm doing really well and you always said that if I discover a hidden talent that I should work to develop it. Well, that is what I am trying to do."

He raises his eyebrows and says, "What I was referring to were real talents, like maybe a sport that you are good at. Speaking of which, did you try out for the basketball team?"

My heart takes another dive. "Tryouts aren't until next week."

"Good. Okay, tell your mother that I said you can have your advance."

"Thanks, Dad!" Well I guess life is full of surprises.

Chapter Six

The next day, outside of the school, Mark shakes his head in disbelief. "I can't believe your dad actually gave you the money. I thought he hated when you played computer games."

"Yeah he does, but it was really pretty easy." Too easy, I think to myself. I know this money comes with a price. Dad didn't say it, but I know he expects something in return; something like trying out for the basketball team. Mom gives me stuff with no strings attached, but it seems like my dad always wants me to earn what he gives me by doing something that *he* wants me to do. And it's usually something I hate doing.

Mark sees the look on my face and asks, "So why do you look so bummed then?"

"My dad is making me try out for the basketball team next week."

Mark laughs. "Stuart Maxwell, school jock. That is hard to imagine."

"Ha-ha. Real funny, Marky. We both know there is absolutely no chance of that happening."

"There goes the bell. I'll catch you later."

We both take off to our first classes. That is one thing I don't like about high school. In junior high, Mark and I were in the same class and had every subject together, but now we have all different classes except for English at the end of the day.

My first class is history and the hour usually flies by because I like history. But what comes next is another thing I don't like about high school: the dreaded gym class. Even though it is an hour long, it feels like it lasts half of the day. I am much better at using my brain than I am at doing anything physical. I am not an A student by any means but I would much rather sit through a boring lecture than put on those baggy gym shorts and run around pretending like I know what I am doing. I would much rather stay here instead but for some strange reason passing four years of gym is mandatory for graduation.

Mrs. Lewis fiddles with her glasses, rubs the indentations they have left on the bridge of her nose, and then checks the time. "Alright, we have time for one more report. Becki Everest, will you please read yours?"

"Yes, Mrs. Lewis."

Becki stands next to her desk shuffling her papers. "History often overlooks the important role women played during this country's past wars. Starting with the American Revolution, women began to make their presence felt. They often were there alongside their fighting men, in the thick of battle, replenishing their ammunition as well their canteens."

Listening to Becki's voice, I can just picture myself there in the midst of battle with my musket, trading volleys of lead with Hessian mercenaries. I fire, and then as I reach into my cartridge box, I find that it is empty! I'm doomed! But wait, who is that running up from the safety of the trees, long blonde hair flying in the wind? It is Becki! In one hand she carries a sack of cartridges; in the other a bucket of water. She stops briefly to hand off some ammo to my companions, bravely ignoring the bullets whizzing within inches of her beautiful face. She drops to her knees in front of me and offers me a drink by dipping a tin cup into the bucket and holding it out to me. I shake my head and gallantly urge her to drink first. She smiles and her bright, blue eyes gaze into mine as she sips from the cup. Then she offers it to me once again and I drink from the side that touched her lips…

Ring! I come out of my daydream with a start. There goes the bell! Ugh! Time for gym class.

There she is, in the hallway right in front of me. I hurry to catch up to her with no real plan in my mind except to talk to her for a minute. "Hey, Becki."

She stops suddenly and turns around right before I get shoved from behind and stumble into her. I know my face is red; I can feel the heat of it. "Oh, sorry." Now I feel stupid for running into her so I don't know what to say. "Um, nice report."

"Thanks."

She is standing there fiddling with the silver quarter moon necklace she always wears, waiting for me to say something else but nothing at all comes to my mind except, "You're welcome."

I hurry away mentally kicking myself. I had the perfect opportunity to start up a civil conversation with her and, as usual, I blew it. I never claimed to be a smooth talker, but I know I can do better than that. I sure hope I can anyway.

———————

Gym class has to be the most useless class in my schedule. Math, Science, English; they all teach you something useful. Even shop class can teach you a trade. What does gym class teach you? How to be a bully to those who aren't as big as you or as good as you are in sports. Every time I walk into the gym it feels like I am entering the monkey house at the zoo. All of the big strong apes pound their chests and chase us weaker little chimps around.

Coach blows his whistle. "Okay, ladies! Line up along the wall. Today we are playing basketball. Todd and Joel will pick the teams. Todd, you're red team."

Great! Mr. Johnson is leaving it up to his favorite athletes to run the class again. Now he will probably ignore us and go work on his playbook while the alpha apes terrorize the rest of us. I hate that they put the freshmen and sophomores together for gym. The sophomores think they are so superior to us just because they are a whole year older.

Joel starts the pick. "I'll take Bob."

"I got Rick."

I hate this. It is just so humiliating. We all know who will get picked first as well as who will be the last ones standing. The last few stragglers, of which I will be one, will be left trying to look cool, as if it doesn't bother us at all that we are considered to be the worst of the worst.

"Steve."

"Mike."

And so on and so on until six of us are left and Joel tells Todd, "Okay, I'll take those three and you can have the other three."

That doesn't do much to boost our self-esteem. They don't even bother to call us by name or even consider who they want on their team more. We are just all equally bad in their opinion.

"Whoa," yells Todd. "That's not fair. You get three and I get two and a half. Stuart Little only counts as half a dude."

Joel laughs. "Yeah, that's a good one."

I hate that nickname! My parents named me Jeb Stuart, after the "greatest light cavalry commander of all time," so why not call me Jeb, which is my real first name? Why did they decide to call me by my middle name that just happens to also be the name of a well-known animated mouse?

Oh great, here we go. I hate basketball. We run around, up and down the court, trying to look like we know what we are doing. It is always the same five or six guys who play the game by themselves while the rest of us are ignored. Even if we should somehow suddenly find the ball in our hands we had better pass it right away to one of the good players. If we don't, then we will get yelled at by our own players, and worse yet we will suffer bodily harm when the other team body checks us and we end up bruised, lying sprawled out on the floor.

I am so tired. I don't know or even care what the score is. Here we go again. I follow them back down to the other basket. Todd has the ball. He wants to shoot but they have him cornered. I am open, so I wave my hands around like I really expect him to throw it to me.

I'm right under the basket now being ignored by the other team since they don't see me as a threat.

Todd sees me. Suddenly he launches the ball directly at me. I defensively throw my hands up to protect my face and by some miracle I actually catch it. What should I do? Give it back to him? Shoot? Everyone is yelling and I hear the sound of many feet charging towards me. I'm right under the basket. Maybe I can make it.

I heave the ball up toward the net, but I have no idea where it went because somebody has slammed into me and sent me skidding across the gym floor. I end up face down, with floor-burned knees and a bump on my chin.

"Foul! Foul," yells Todd. He sounds mad. "Two free throws!"

"Whatever," Joel sneers. "He can't make a basket to save his life anyway."

Todd comes over and lifts me up by the back of my shirt. "Alright, get up. You get two free throws and you better make at least one of them. That will tie us up and we can go into overtime. Make the shot, or else!"

Thanks for your concern! My knees hurt, and I think my tongue is bleeding from biting it when I smacked my chin.

"Stand here, and don't step over that line!"

They line up on either side of me, arms spread wide and with knees bent, waiting to pounce. Well, here it goes.

I give the ball a couple of practice bounces like I have seen the others do. Gaze up intently at the net. Bend my knees; *ouch, that hurts!* Quickly I spring into action, letting the ball fly from my hands. Good, I stayed behind the foul line.

Darn! I missed. It didn't even hit the backboard. Everyone is laughing, even some of my own team members. Todd is glaring at me, probably trying to kill me with his mind.

I get one more shot. Why should I even try? I'm no good at this. I bounce the ball once, twice, three times.

"Come on dork. Shoot!"

"Yeah, come on!"

Okay, here goes nothing.

Laughter erupts in the gym. The basketball is stuck on top of the backboard. Wow; I just stand there marveling at the fact that I actually threw the ball so close to the basket. At least I hit the backboard this time. Then I see Todd coming toward me.

"Way to go, moron, you cost us the game."

Ouch! He didn't have to elbow me in the ribs. I try not to think about the fact that I will have to face him at tryouts too. I wouldn't go, except, if I don't, Dad will probably ban me from video games for the rest of my life.

Chapter Seven

Friday is here at last! Since the game starts at four o'clock I have made sure to get my homework done at school. My room is clean, or as clean as it is going to be without me getting in trouble. I have the credit card information. The computer is hooked up to the TV. All I need to do now is log in and wait.

> Greetings Number 49215. Your mission today is to travel back to the year 1943 where you will provide air cover for a German armored unit on the Eastern Front. Your team member is Number 89264. Together you will proceed to the nearest German airfield where you will each choose your mount.

Number 89264? I guess they aren't going to assign us names this time. I like that though. Every game is different in some way. Sometimes they give us our name, sometimes we name ourselves, and other times we get to name each other.

I have never had this partner before but he must be good if he has made it this far. His ID number is pretty high. I wonder if there have been 89263 players before him?

I should be really good at this game. I may not excel at sports but I do know my history, especially military history.

The portal opens and I am through. I walk across the grass strip that is the German airbase. In my hand is a copy of my mission map. Marked in black are the German Panzer tanks and Panzer Grenadier halftracks that I have been assigned to protect. Highlighted in red are the known enemy Russian tank and infantry regiments. Wow, there are so many of them!

I see a row of aircraft in the tree line. The first one that catches my eye is the Ju-87 Stuka. I recognize it by its inverted-gull-wings and spat covered, fixed landing gear. The two wicked, 37 mm anti-tank guns slung under each wing give it the appearance of a flying scorpion. Although it is one of my favorite aircraft, and a most potent tank destroyer, I know this is not the ideal airplane to carry out my mission.

Another German pilot approaches me. He is tall with black hair and a thin moustache. He kind of reminds me of Adolf Galland, the German Ace, and Knight's Cross recipient.

He extends his hand and says, "Greetings Number 49215. Is this your first tour here on the Eastern Front?"

"Yes," I reply. I'm feeling fairly confident. I know my World War II aircraft pretty well. I have built and painted a lot of models too, but I better not mention that to him. The last thing I would want him to know is that his teammate is a kid.

We stroll among the various planes intent on making the right choice. The Stuka dive bomber has been modified as a tank destroyer. The cannons look awesome, and are deadly against tanks, but the guns are slow firing with limited ammunition. This is not the ideal choice for dogfighting with other planes.

Sitting next to the Stuka is a ME-110, a twin engine, multi-role fighter-bomber. This one has a lot going for it. The multiple antennas stuck all over the front of it are airborne radar that would help us find our targets. It carries a powerful battery of guns that would enable us to destroy just about any enemy aircraft we came across. The only drawback is that it cannot maneuver as well as a fighter, nor is it as fast. If we run into some Migs, or Yaks, we would be in trouble.

The next beauty that draws my attention is a Me-109, the favorite of Erich Hartmann, with 352 confirmed victories. He was, and is, the highest scoring ace of all time. I do believe this is the G-6 model. It has a 30 mm cannon that fires through the propeller hub, two 13 mm heavy machine guns mounted above the engine, and a 15 mm cannon under each wing. That is a lot of heavy firepower with the maneuverability of a single engine fighter.

The last one is the Fw-190. I am pretty sure this one carries two 13 mm above the engine and two 20 mm cannon in each wing. It has good speed but is not as maneuverable at low levels as the Me-109.

My partner makes his decision. "I think I'll give the Me-109 a go. What about you?"

I think he has made a wise choice. I feel better knowing that he must have good knowledge about these aircraft too.

I was originally going to opt for the Fw-190, because that way I could fly overhead cover for him and have the advantage of speed and height. But after reconsidering, I change my mind. Both the Me-109 and Fw-190 are good airplanes, but what good are they if we cannot locate the targets?

Having made my choice, I answer with, "I choose the Me-110 with the radar capabilities. That way I can find the targets, and then we can take them out together. I may need to rely on you to help me if we tangle with Soviet fighters. Can I trust you to watch my back?" It was a legitimate question in light of Badger's betrayal in the past game.

"That is a good plan," he responds. "Yes, if you fly the 110, I promise to watch your back."

We shake hands and part ways to check out our aircraft.

The Me-110 was good in its day when it was used as a bomber destroyer, and it was especially deadly as a night fighter.

As I approach the ladder on the trailing edge of the port wing I see my radar operator is already strapped into the rear seat. "Greetings, sir. I am Lieutenant Hess. I will be your radar operator today," he says as I climb aboard.

I find it ironic that they gave me a radar operator named Hess since Rudolf Hess was the name of Adolph Hitler's right hand man until he unexpectedly flew off to Scotland in a Me-110.

"It looks like a fine day for hunting," I quip as I strap myself in and look around. The cockpit layout looks like your standard cockpit; a confusing mass of dials, knobs, and switches. Lucky for me, my character is equipped with the basic knowledge to be able to start up and fly the aircraft. The ground crew closes my canopy and removes the blocks from the wheels. I wave back to them as I begin to taxi out onto the field.

I see the Me-109 swing out slightly behind me as player number 89264 follows me out. We begin our takeoff run and pass by the anti-aircraft guns defending the airfield. The twin 12-cylinder Daimler-Benz engines roar as we climb into the sky scattering the sheep that have been 'mowing' the field. Leaving the earth behind, I raise the landing gear.

Almost immediately Hess informs me that he has received a radio message saying that Soviet Pe-2 dive bombers have been sighted passing over the lines in sector two. That has to be our first target so I pull back on the stick and we begin to climb into the clouds.

Hess turns on the radar. My wingman, number 89264, is still on my tail so I call him on the radio.

"Hartmann, this is 49215, do you copy?"

"This is Hartmann. I copy." Evidently he accepts the fact that I just christened him Hartmann after the famous German Ace pilot. Besides, that will be much easier than calling him by his gamer number.

"We have just received a radio message that Russian dive bombers have been sighted. My guess is that they will be hiding in the clouds. We will begin searching with our radar. Close in and stay close to me."

"Roger that, Snoopy," Hartmann responds.

Snoopy? Ha-ha, that's a good one! How ironic that he has christened me after Charlie Brown's dog who likes to pretend that he is a famous British World War I flying ace. Snoopy imagines that his doghouse is a Sopwith Camel fighter plane that he flies over the trenches in no-man's-land searching for and doing battle with the German ace known as the Red Baron. And now here I am a World War II German ace named Snoopy. Darn, I wish I would have thought to call him Red Baron.

Hess tells me that we have a contact. Dead ahead, bearing three, four, zero. The radar is showing four aircraft directly ahead of us. They must not know we are here since they don't seem to be taking any evasive action.

"Hartmann, I will take the two on the left, you go for the ones on the right."

"Roger, Snoopy."

I realize that this version of the Pe-2 may be armed with both 12.7 mm and 7.62 mm machineguns, on both top and bottom side. There may also be 20 mm guns in the wings for firing ahead for strafing. This is going to be tricky.

The clouds suddenly part and there are the enemy planes right in front of us. Since the Pe-2 is a twin engine plane like my own, plus it is carrying a heavy bomb load, I should not have to worry about them out maneuvering me. As we close in, one of their rear gunners spot us, and a lazy arch of tracer bullets seek us out. Not wasting any time, I hit the firing button and send some cannon shells his way. Yes! I'm right on target. Their left engine explodes into a ball of fire and there is a loud crack as his wing falls off. As I swing my nose around to train the guns on my next target I see that Hartmann has also been successful at destroying one of their planes.

The tracer bullets from my next intended victim are coming dangerously close to me. I fire a quick burst of my own but it fails to bring him down. This time I take a deep breath and aim more carefully. Just as I fire again, my aircraft starts taking hits from the Pe-2 gunners. My aim is better this time and I'm relieved to see pieces start to fall off the Pe-2. My palms are getting sweaty from the tension. Determined not to let them take me down, I fire again and the defensive guns that have been pelting my craft go silent. Still, I don't take my eyes off of it until I see that the damage I have caused it is complete. The destroyed enemy aircraft noses over and falls to the earth in a mass of twisted metal, exploding as it hits the ground.

Only now do I have a second to check to see how my partner is fairing. Satisfied that his second target is also going down I start searching the skies for the Pe-2 escorts. They have to be here somewhere.

I circle around while Hess uses the radar to check for enemy aircraft hidden in the clouds. True to his word to 'watch my back,' Hartmann circles around to get behind my wing.

Suddenly I spot them, dead ahead and closing fast. There are two of them. No, three. Four. Coming straight for us now!

I radio Hartmann to tell him that I will take the two on the left again but before he can answer, bullets are peppering our planes sounding like popcorn popping over a campfire. We fire our cannons as fast as we can in response to their attack.

Bang! A Soviet 7.62 mm bullet hits my protective bullet proof glass leaving a mark that resembles a snowflake. Thankfully it doesn't penetrate the thick glass and I am safe.

Yes! One of my cannon shells hits its mark and my opponent's canopy explodes. A few inches of bulletproof glass cannot stand up to one of my 30 mm cannon rounds.

I zip past the other fighter so fast that I cannot make out what kind it is. I head for the clouds so I can figure out my next move. I climb hard and disappear from sight before the Russian fighter can come around to get on my tail. I catch a glimpse of Hartmann in the foggy mist. We can't stay hidden for long. There is always the danger of colliding with an enemy plane that might have had the same idea as we did. Also the clock is ticking down. We have to complete our mission before the time runs out or we will be eliminated from playing future games.

All is quiet for a few seconds as we each get our bearings. I hear Hartmann's voice in the earphones cursing, after nearly ramming into one of the Russian fighters in the clouds.

I drop down a little so I can see better, and get lucky. Directly in front of me is an enemy plane so I pour on the power. My engines are straining to give me a little extra speed. Slowly I sneak up underneath him. He starts into a turn as he searches for a target and I am able to gain on him a little more. Being below him and to his rear I know he cannot see me. It is his one blind spot. I now recognize his silhouette; my enemy is a Yak-1.

Ever so slowly I slide into position. We are completely clear of the cloud cover now. If he spots me, or if his comrade suddenly appears, Hess and I are dead men. There is no place to hide and we cannot outrun them.

I am totally focused on my target. I ease in a little closer hardly daring to breathe I am concentrating so intently. Almost there…Now!

I fire the two 30 mm cannon that are pointed upwards and at a forward angle. These *Schrage Musik* cannon are designed for ripping the belly out of an unsuspecting bomber at night. Alright! I did it! The little Russian fighter explodes and plummets to earth.

I bank and head back for the clouds to find out how Hartmann is doing. He answers me with frustration in his voice.

"Twice now I have nearly rammed into that persistent Russian here in the clouds. He is in here somewhere circling around me, playing a game of cat and mouse."

I consult with Hess. He gives me an update and I relay the information to Hartmann. "Hartmann, Hess sees two blips on his radar screen heading directly for each other." This can only mean that Hartmann is just moments away from crashing head on into the last remaining fighter. "Can you see anything?" I ask. I have to help him to survive. If he dies then I may not have the firepower to finish this on my own which would be the end of me too.

"Negative," he answers. "I can't see a thing."

"Okay then," I say, trying to keep calm. "Since you are flying blind I will have to be your eyes. Hess can see what is happening on the radar screen. Keep flying straight ahead and when I tell you to, fire a quick burst and then roll sharply to the right."

Boy, I sure hope this works. Everything depends on this and the timing has to be perfect.

"Ready…Now!" I yell into the microphone.

Except for the sound of our engines, all is silent. I can't see what is happening and the suspense is killing me.

A few seconds later Hartmann calls out triumphantly, "I see a parachute!"

We are all cheering and congratulating each other when a voice comes over the radio with a report of Stormoviks passing over our lines at low level in Sector 6. I should have known the game wouldn't be this easy! Our job is not over yet. We must stop the Stormoviks before they reach our tanks. All it would take is one pass by the Stormovik ground attack planes to wipe out every one of our armored vehicles with their 23 mm cannon and PTAB cluster bombs. We must take them out on the first pass. Their planes are heavily armored and they are the model with the rear gunners. It will be tricky but we do have a chance as long as we make no mistakes. If all goes well, our cannon should be able to punch through their armor.

We begin diving down when my eye catches a reflection of sunlight off of a Russian aircraft canopy. Luck is on our side, for not only have we found them, but we are diving in on them from out of the sun. The old World War I saying comes to my mind, *Beware of the Hun in the sun!* Our German fighters with the bright sun behind us remain undetected by the Stormoviks. There are only two of them, but those two can do a lot of damage.

On the ground in the distance I see our Panzer tanks moving slowly forward in a wedge formation like a herd of armored turtles plodding along through the standing wheat. Crawling behind them are the halftracks carrying the Panzer Grenadiers.

Fortunately we have built up a pretty good airspeed in our dive. I call Hartmann. "Are you ready for some action?" I ask excitedly.

"Roger that Snoopy," he answers, sounding as excited as I am.

We quickly close in on the low flying tank busters. At the last minute their gunners spot us and we all open fire at the same time. My twin cannon shells hit all over the doomed Stormovik and he noses over drunkenly and crashes into the ground.

Ha-ha! One down! I just hope Hartmann is successful in taking his down too. As I circle around above, I see Hartmann's shells striking home right into the enemy's engine. There is a small explosion on the front of the Stormovik and its spinning propeller separates from the plane. A moment later the crippled plane spirals down as if in slow motion and plows into a hedgerow, raising a huge cloud of dust.

"That was a close one," announces Hartmann. "And I am out of ammo."

I check my own cannon round indicator and find that both of my nose guns are also empty. Well hopefully we won't need them now. It looks like we have cleared the skies of enemy planes and our men below are free and clear.

We fly over our comrades on the ground and we can see them waving and cheering so we rock our wings in reply. Only now do I realize how tightly I have been gripping my controller. I flex my stiff fingers and wait to find out my score. I think it should be a pretty good one. Hopefully it will be high enough for me to be able to move on.

But wait! The game's not over yet? There is something concealed in the tree line up ahead of our troops. I look closer, squinting my eyes to bring them into better focus, and I can just make out a string of enemy guns. An ambush! Our men are heading right into a trap! There is no way to warn them and I can only watch helplessly as our troops advance closer and closer to the enemy's guns. I have to do something.

I make a split second decision with no time to tell Hartmann what I plan to do. I line up my plane to make a pass directly over the waiting Russian guns. As I bear down on them, I see the enemy gunners looking up at me. I am out of cannon shells for my nose guns but I have an idea. I'm not sure if it will work or not, but I figure that it might be worth trying. Right before I fly over the first gun I roll the Me-110 over on its back and fire the *Schrage Musik* that were pointing at an upward angle but are now pointing downward. I am so close, I can see the looks of fear on the faces of the Soviet gunners as they realize what I am about to do. I leave a trail of explosions behind me as I make my pass. Some of the surviving Russian infantry are firing their submachine guns at me and I can hear the impact of their bullets striking my craft.

I flip the plane right side up and look back over my shoulder. I can't see what is happening down below but I can see that Hartmann is behind me, true to his word to back me up.

"Holy cow, Snoopy! That was something," exclaims Hartmann.

"GAME OVER!"

Well done Number 49215. The German infantry has been deployed to deal with the remaining Russian guns. You took out three enemy guns and were successful in alerting your ground troops to the impending trap.

Oh my gosh! Not only did I get the maximum allowable coins for defending against air attack, but I got extra coins for taking out anti-tank guns too. I wonder what Hartmann got? I hope I scored better than he did. I just gotta move on to the next game!

I hear the sound of someone leaving the room. Was that Mom watching me play? No, I forgot, she's at her pottery class. The only other person here is my dad. That's weird. Oh well, I guess he probably came in to see if I was done with the TV, or to get his glasses or something.

Chapter Eight

It sure seems strange for Becki to not be at my bus stop anymore since she had to move out of the neighborhood. From the time that I started at this school she has been here, usually the first to arrive. Life was so much easier when we were in grade school. Back then I could talk to her as much as I wanted as long as I was calling her names or teasing her. I could just pull off her knit hat and she would be chasing me all over trying to get it back. And if I was lucky, she would catch me and sit on my chest until I surrendered it back to her. That was a way to let someone know that you liked them without actually having to come right out and tell them. At least that is how it was when we were younger.

I'm too old for that kind of stuff now. If I did something like that now, she might start crying and then I would feel like a jerk. Now that we are freshmen in high school, I don't know how to talk to her. I sure do like her but when I try to start a conversation with her, I usually end up embarrassed and sounding like a dork.

It would be easy to let her know how I feel about her if we lived back in the olden days. If I was a brave knight and she was a princess, I could show her how I felt by championing her on the tournament jousting field. She would be seated next to her father, the king, under a pavilion in her pale blue dress that matched her eyes exactly, and with a crown of white flowers on her head.

I ride my sleek white charger over to her and she favors me with a brilliant smile. The heraldry on my shield and surcoat is the same blue as her dress and eyes. I lift the visor of my helmet and bow my head to her father. "For your daughter's favor will I do battle," I boldly announce.

She honors me by taking her delicately embroidered handkerchief and presenting it for me to attach to my lance. My heart lifts as she says, "Now everyone will know you are mine. May God be with you, my champion."

I turn my steed and trot over to take my place at the opposite end of the field from the Black Knight. As menacing as he looks in all black armor sitting on his jet black warhorse, I am not afraid. I lower my visor and ready my lance. My great warhorse snorts and his hooves scratch at the earth, showing his impatience. The trumpet sounds and I spur my horse forward. I have no fear for I can hear Princess Becki cheering me on.

"Hey Stuart, how's it going?"

I snap out of my daydream with a start. "Hey Mark, I didn't think you were going to make it before the bus came."

Mark makes a disgusted face. "It was my sister again."
"Kim?"

"Duh, who else?" he laughs. Imitating his sister, he says in a high squeaky voice. "She's like, 'I need to get in the bathroom to fix my hair!' So," he continues in a normal tone, "she hogs the bathroom, and while she is supposed to be doing her hair, I hear her stupid phone beeping because she's in there texting. Man, just be glad you don't have an older sister, especially one who is a popular cheerleader."

Changing the subject he asks, "So what are you up to? You sure were thinking hard when I got here."

"I was just thinking about my history report," I lie. "It's due today, but I'm not quite done with it yet."

"You should ask Becki to help you," Mark offers, with a grin stretched across his face.

"What is that supposed to mean?"

He sees my indignant frown and laughs. "Hey, I'm just saying she is good at history. Man, don't have a cow!"

I know he is just being a smart aleck, but the truth is I would love to have Becki help me with my report, homework, or anything else. It's just that I am too nervous to ask her. Just as this conversation is getting uncomfortable, I'm saved by the arrival of our bus.

Climbing the bus steps and starting down the aisle, I am already searching her out. Mark got on first so I have time to look without him on my heels rushing me. He is always in a hurry to find a seat for us so we can sit together. There she is, towards the back.

Before I can build up the nerve to even decide if today is the day that I will sit by Becki, Mark has found a spot a couple of rows up and across the aisle from her. He plops down and yanks on my arm so I have no choice but to chicken out and sink down next to him.

Right away he starts up with his latest news. "I talked to my grandma and she is going to get me that new game I wanted for my birthday."

"Cool," I say. "You'll have to let me know how it is when you get it."

As Mark rattles on about the new game he is getting, I try to listen like a good friend but my mind slowly slips to the rear of the bus where Becki sits. I take a quick look back and see her staring out of the dirty window. While the other kids are yelling, texting, or talking to each other she just sits there quietly alone. I wonder what she is thinking about.

I feel bad for her. She used to have lots of friends before her family lost their house and money. Now those "friends" avoid her and make fun of her behind her back and sometimes even right to her face.

"So what do you think I should do?" Mark asks.

Before I can let on that I wasn't listening to him, the bus is making its dreaded last stop. This is the stop on the route where Todd's younger brother Derik gets on. Where Todd is a sophomore and the high school jock and bully, Derik is the terror of the junior high and unfortunately, the school bus. He is only a seventh grader but he is bigger than I am and he has no problem being just as big a bully as his older brother. Do you know how humiliating it is to be picked on by someone two years younger than you are?

Everyone was happy and relieved when Todd got his driver's license and started driving himself and his brother to school. But now his mean little clone takes the bus because Todd wants to be at school early for basketball practice.

Here he comes down the aisle yelling the usual greetings and insults to his friends and his victims. As he passes by, I get a hard punch in the arm and an insult as he says, "Hey it's Stuart Little. I almost didn't see you there little fella." His buddies laugh like he has said the funniest thing they have ever heard.

"Leave him alone, Derik," warns Mark.

Derik gives him an obscene gesture and keeps on moving without answering. It isn't that Mark is such a tough guy that Derik is afraid of him; far from it. But Derik *is* afraid of Todd and Todd has a major crush on Mark's sister Kim. Todd would squash his brother like the insect he is, if he messed things up for him by bullying Kim's little brother. That is the only reason that I am usually safer from both Derik and Todd when Mark is around.

I resist the urge to rub my arm where he punched me. Man, that hurt, but I play it cool and pretend it didn't. I am already embarrassed enough, being picked on by a seventh grader. I just hope Becki didn't see it. I don't think I will try talking to her today. Besides, I am already nervous enough with tryouts starting later.

———

Tryouts. Why do they even call it that? They already know who they want on the team. There's Todd talking to Coach Johnson, probably going over the playbook. Maybe Todd will be so preoccupied with that, he will forget about what happened last week in gym class. *Don't make eye contact...* Oh shoot, why did I look at him? He looked right at me and I can tell from his nasty glare that he hasn't forgotten anything.

The assistant coach, Mr. Dunbar, is calling us over. Well, I might as well get it over with.

"All right ladies, twice around the field and then fall back in here. Go! We haven't got all day! Get going!"

They expect us to run outside first? Unbelievable! I will be too tired out to do anything afterwards. And twice around the field must be five miles!

Thank goodness tryouts are over with. This has been the longest two hours of my life! I can't believe it is finally done with and I get to go home. For the life of me I cannot understand why anybody would *want* to do that. I hurt all over. My knees are still bruised from last week. My leg muscles are sore from running. My ribs ache from breathing so hard. My arm hurts from Derik's punch. My hands are sore from handling the rough basketball, plus I jammed a finger. I hate this. I sure hope I didn't make the cut. Well at least I can honestly tell my dad that I tried. I wriggle my fingers and wince in pain. I better be able to use my hands for the video game on Friday.

Chapter Nine

Greetings Number 49215. Your mission today is to travel forward in time to the year 2027 where you are to perform a rescue mission. A plague has infected a small portion of the population, with those individuals being quarantined on a deserted island. As per UN mandate no one is allowed to go in, and certainly no person is allowed to leave.

A small plane carrying the children of a wealthy client has crash landed on this forbidden land mass. A brief message has been received stating that the two children are believed to still be alive. Your mission is to find these children and bring them back through the UN blockade.

You have fifteen minutes to complete this task.

Fifteen minutes? You have got to be kidding me! That doesn't give me much time at all. It does sound interesting but they don't specify what the plague they are referring to is. I guess I am supposed to figure it out for myself.

I flex my fingers and feel confident that they are up for the task. Okay, here goes nothing.

Walking along the sandy beach I spot a boat partially hidden in some bushes. I am wearing head to toe flexible body armor and I have holstered pistols strapped to each of my thighs and both forearms. Slung over my shoulder is a small assault rifle equipped with a silencer. Huh, that's interesting. Well, I guess the silencer is to avoid waking the neighborhood and drawing the attention of every plague ridden person on the island to me. My sheathed knife is strapped to my calf, binoculars are slung around my neck, and a stun gun rests on one hip. Oh, cool! I see one of the items in my inventory is a set of plastic tie handcuffs. Handcuffs for a couple of kids? Well maybe if the kids were Todd and Derik. I smile to myself at that thought.

Also in my inventory are a compass and a message. I better check the message out first. There is no telling what helpful bit of information I might find. Hah, I was right. It is a brief description of the plane-wrecked kids. There is a boy named Philip, age eight, and a girl, Suzanne, who is thirteen. They are wearing school uniforms of green and yellow plaid and white shirts. Both are dark haired with brown eyes. A satellite image has pinpointed them entering a small church not far north of where I am now. I retrieve the compass and get moving.

As I make my way through the brush I spot some footprints in the dirt. They look small enough to have been made by children. So far so good, but just to be on the safe side I get my assault rifle with the silencer ready. I will use it first if I have to, and then the knife, since I need to be as quiet as I can. I will save the pistols for last.

I catch sight of a small dilapidated church through the trees. The once whitewashed walls are stained and faded and the roof is rotted and sagging. It looks sad and neglected. I pause for a moment to look around. There is a four-foot, spiked, wrought-iron fence surrounding the building but luckily the gate is wide open. There is an occasional bush scattered about the yard and a cluster of them on the left side of the building. I work my way around using the bushes for cover until I reach the rear of the church.

Good, I've made it without seeing anyone. I approach the back door and gently nudge it open with the barrel of my rifle. The old hinges creak, but they easily give way. Slowly the door opens allowing the sunlight to shine a hazy path through the dust and gloom. I step into the small foyer and listen for sounds of life, but I hear nothing.

As I start to move, I hear a noise from inside and freeze. Footsteps! Someone is coming this way from the next room. Quickly I slip into the shadows and pull out my knife. As the footsteps draw nearer I prepare to strike.

Just as I am ready to jump out for the attack, a beautiful young woman enters the room. She has long, black hair, and is wearing wooden clogs, very short cutoffs, and a flannel shirt with the shirt tails tied neatly around her small waist. I stand out of her line of sight, wondering what I should do. She keeps looking all around her like a nervous squirrel. Just as I decide to make my presence known, she turns around and sees me. A look of fear crosses her face and she screams in fright. Bolting past me, she runs out the back door.

In a flash and without thinking it through, I am out there chasing after her. Maybe she has information that can help me find the kids, or at the very least perhaps she can join me in my search.

I chase her around the building to the front where she has lost her clunky shoes enabling her to scamper quick as a rabbit now while I am bogged down and hindered by my gear. She reaches a large, old gnarled tree and ducks behind it. I can see her peeking around it at me seconds before she takes off running once again. Finally I am gaining on her as she approaches the iron fence.

She is cornered with nowhere to escape to. "Stop," I call, trying to sound friendly. "I won't hurt you. I just want to talk to you."

She hesitates just long enough for me to catch up to her before she leaps over the fence in a single bound. As she lands on the opposite side, her body transforms into a black mist right before it disappears altogether into thin air.

I stop dead in my tracks. How could I be so stupid! She must have just been a diversion to make me use up precious time, and I fell for it. Three minutes into the game already and I have accomplished nothing. I run back to the rear door only to find that it is now closed and locked tight. Darn, now I have to waste more time finding another way in. I check each window as I work my way around to the front. Each one is tightly sealed and the grimy stained glass is impossible to see through. Cautiously, I peer around the front corner of the building and look toward the double front doors. Now I have no choice but to try to go in through the front way.

But wait…There is a tangled mass of vines growing up the side of the church. I grab onto a fistful of twisted leaves and am able to climb all the way to the roof and drop in through the open-sided bell tower.

Good, it's empty. Pulling out my binoculars, I look out into the distance where there are some people moving about. Everybody appears to be normal enough. I wonder what the plague could be. I decide to stay away from everyone until I figure out what I am dealing with.

Standing at the top of the stairway leading down to the main floor I can hear shuffling sounds and whispering down below. It could be the children, but then again it may not be. I take one careful step onto the first wooden stair. It creaks and groans under my weight. I stop to listen but all is now silent. With my rifle barrel pointing the way, I continue down to the main floor.

The room is empty but again I hear noises coming from behind a closed door. I ease it open a couple of inches and peek in. There are rows of dusty old benches and an altar but I don't see any sign of people. "Suzanne,

Philip?" I whisper. "Are you in here? Don't be afraid, I have been sent to rescue you."

In the dim light, I see a young girl stand up between two of the benches. Rising up beside her is a smaller child. As my eyes adjust to the gloom, I can see that their clothes are tattered and filthy dirty but it looks like their clothing could have been school uniforms. I feel somewhat relieved but I don't lower my rifle. I still have to get them out of here safely, but something seems fishy.

I approach the two kids warily. As soon as I get a few feet from them, the girl lets out a blood curdling screech and throws herself at me. She is smaller than I am but very strong. The impact knocks me down and we roll around on the floor while I try to get a good grip on her in order to pin her down. She is going crazy, screaming and gnashing her teeth trying to bite me. Zombie! She's a zombie! That's what the plague is.

No matter what, I cannot destroy her because my assignment is to rescue them. I finally manage to hold her down long enough to whip out my stun gun. Leaping up off of her I take careful aim and pull the trigger. Zap! Her body spasms a couple of times before she is rendered immobile and temporarily paralyzed. Hearing a sound from behind, I spin around to see the young boy coming at me with the same blank stare and lust for blood as his sister. A swift kick to the chest sends him stumbling back and I run out of the room and slam the door shut putting my shoulder to it while I brace myself and try to figure this one out.

Unfortunately, the children that I was sent to rescue have both already become infected. From what I know about zombies, those two must have already been bitten, died, and turned. Maybe that was why I was given the stun gun and plastic tie handcuffs. Maybe the real challenge is to bring the zombified kids back 'alive' without becoming infected myself. If that is the case, it's a good thing that I only shot the girl with the stun gun and didn't blow her head off with the rifle. I'm sure the family would prefer to have their kids returned with their heads still intact.

They are scratching and clawing at the door I am holding shut and making sounds like wounded animals. I sling my rifle over my shoulder and grip my stun gun as I prepare to face them once again. I open the door just wide enough for their thin diseased arms to reach through. I zap the bigger arm until it shakes, goes limp, and disappears and then I do the same with the smaller one. After a couple of seconds, I open the door a bit more and look in. Both of them are lying on the floor motionless.

I have to move fast now. Pulling out the plastic cuffs, I secure the children's hands behind their backs. I manage to pick up both of them and sling one over each shoulder. With my little load secured and balanced, I head back to the beach at a trot.

I run to the small partially concealed boat to make my escape from the island. I am very aware of the timer ticking down in the bottom corner of the screen. Seven minutes in now with only eight left to go.

Just as I reach the boat the kids start to move around. I drop them down in the sand and drag the rubber boat with outboard engine to the water's edge. The kids are coming around but are still a little groggy. Not wanting to babysit a couple of zombie brats while trying to drive the boat through the rough seas, I zap each one again. Ha ha, take that you little monsters!

I notice three children standing in the distant tree line staring at us. They seem normal enough; unlike these two creepy Chucky dolls, but I can't waste any of my precious time in chasing them down.

A woman appears with arms spread wide, gathering the three together and leading them quickly away like a mother hen protecting her young chicks. I can't blame her. If I was her, I would run in the opposite direction too if I saw these kids.

After loading my cargo of dead weight; or would that be, 'undead' weight? I launch the boat and head out at full speed to the open sea. There is a fishing boat chugging lazily along and I make a split second decision to head for it. It may or may not be in this game for a reason but I have to check it out just in case.

I secure my boat and hop on board, looking back to make sure the zombie kids are still out of it, when suddenly I hear movement behind me. A male zombie is hobbling quickly toward me with a large knife in his raised hand. He is moving unusually fast for an undead so when he actually lunges at me I am almost caught off guard. I didn't know they could move so quickly, and I never knew of a zombie to use a weapon to attack. I dodge the long sharp blade and bring up one of my own which punctures the side of his skull above his right ear. Like a good zombie, he goes down.

Not taking any chances, I ready my rifle. Two more undead appear and I easily dispatch of each of them by blowing major holes in their heads. All is quiet for the moment so I quickly carry my two little freaks aboard and tie them up securely. I cut my boat free, shove the destroyed zombies into the water and head further out to sea. I should make better time in this vessel and once I clear the UN blockade I should be relieved of my creepy cargo. I just hope I have enough time left to finish.

A naval patrol craft has spotted me and is closing in. I better not try to turn and flee. They could easily catch up to my fishing vessel or they can sink us with gunfire, so I keep on my course and wait to see what happens.

They pull alongside of me and I kill the engine. Two of them climb aboard my boat and tie the ships together. They are being covered by a soldier manning a machinegun. It looks like a big gun; a .50 caliber. When I get a better look at them all I realize that they too are zombies!

I snatch up my rifle and shoot the one manning the machinegun first, aiming for his head. Then I quickly take out the other two. There is no time to waste as I leap aboard the naval ship. Another creature appears out of a hatchway and I kill him with the last round from my rifle. Time to draw my pistols.

I pull out my .45 caliber in time to take out two crewmen carrying guns. Two head shots take care of both of them. I hear the crack of a pistol and a slug grazes my shoulder armor. Spinning around I fire wildly wasting ammunition before I calm down enough to aim properly. Hah, take that creep! Right between the eyes! He twirls around like a one-legged ballerina before falling over the ship's railing.

Two minutes left! I have to move fast. I run up the stairs to the wheel house and fire my last round into the crewman manning the wheel. Immediately, I whip out my 9 mm, kick in the door of the radio room, and take out the ugly dude wearing the headphones. Racing back on deck I spy three soldiers who are distracted by something going on behind them. This is my chance. Running forward and weaving from side to side I close the distance as I empty my clip into them. The ship is mine!

Only then do I take a second to glance at the timer. Thirty seconds left? I can't believe I lost this one. I walk over to the side of the ship where the soldiers had been looking and I see a small submersible type of mini submarine. The hatch is open and two adult zombies, one male and one female, have boarded the ship. I raise my last remaining pistol and center the male in my gun sight but just as I am about to pull the trigger the female lets out a cry and runs to the little zombie children, cuts their ties and starts hugging them like crazy. The male then looks over at me and raises his hand as if in greeting and nods his head in thanks.

I drop my gun hand to my side. "What the heck?" Do you mean to tell me that the zombies were the ones who hired me to rescue their children from the plague-infested island? That would mean that the zombies are the normal ones here and the people quarantined on the island, who really are normal, were the infected ones?

"GAME OVER!"

While I wait for the results, I try to figure everything out. I have never played a game that messed with my brain like this. Usually I just play, react, and find things out by hit or miss.

So if the zombies were considered to be normal, and the infected ones were sent to the island, the question is why send them to the island instead of just killing them to turn them into zombies too? Unless…If everything is the opposite then maybe the humans wouldn't be turned; instead maybe it is the zombies that would be turned to human and then they would have to be sent to the island too. Yes! That would explain why all of the creatures used weapons against me instead of just biting me, because then they would have become infected. The two kids, being young, didn't understand this, which would be why they tried to attack me the only way they knew how; by biting.

> Congratulations number 49215. You have successfully completed your mission in the allotted amount of time. You have returned the children to their parents and saved them from becoming infected and turned to human form where they would have been forced to be separated from their family forever. As members of the human race, they would have been subjected to suffering human pain and

illness, until eventually reaching that final agonizing state of no return, called death.

You have received 700 gold coins and the opportunity to participate in our next game.

So I was right. I guess they believed it was better to be a zombie because as an undead, they didn't have to feel pain, or experience sickness and death. And of course, zombies "live" forever. Unless of course, you blow their heads off.

Chapter Ten

I still haven't heard who made the final cut for the basketball team; the team that I don't even want to be on. My body type and size is just not made for sports. Now if I had a body like one of my computer characters, then that would be a different story. I probably still wouldn't be interested in sports but at least I would know that I could do it if I wanted to. If I had a build like Mandor, guys like Todd and Derik would be afraid to mess with me and girls would be flirting with me, trying to get me to like them. But even though I could have my choice of any girl in the whole school, I would make it clear to all of them that the only girl I was interested in is Becki.

As it is now, if I was trying out for something like the chess club, where I had to use brains instead of brawn, then I would have a fighting chance, that is, if I even wanted to compete on the chess team, which I don't.

Even though chess is a strategy game, I don't care for it. I know guys like Todd think I'm a loser just because I can't play ball like him, but the truth is, I think the chess club members are a bunch of nerds. Personally, I think those Poindexters are further down the geek chain than I ever was. For all of their brains, I sometimes have to feel sorry for them. I guess some people were born to be bullies and others were born to be their unfortunate victims.

Take Humphrey Dempsey, for example. Now who would be cruel enough to name their kid Humphrey in this day and age? In this school, you may as well be wearing a sign that says, "Kick me!" I have nothing against the poor guy but even if I didn't like him, I would just leave him alone. But people like Todd and Derik aren't like me. They are more like an attack dog that cannot resist the temptation when they sniff out someone weaker or more passive than they are.

Heading for my locker in between classes, I see Todd has Humphrey in his sights right now.

"Come on Humpty Dumpty, if you want your book back, come and get it."

"Please give me my book, I need it for class," pleads small, skinny Humphrey with the pop-bottle-thick glasses.

I hate watching this and cannot understand why nobody is helping the kid.

"Hey Kim!" Todd yells to get her attention as he sends the textbook flying to one of his buddies. His partner in crime misses the catch and it nearly loses its binding as it tumbles down the hallway.

Standing in front of her open locker surrounded by her friends, Mark's sister, Kim, glances his way and smiles, but then flips her hair over her shoulder and turns back to check her reflection in the mirror hanging on her locker door. Being a cheerleader, she has to make sure her hair and makeup is always just right. And it always is.

Even though Todd is a year younger than she is, everyone knows he has a major crush on her. Since she is a popular junior, dating a sophomore would be beneath her. To her, he is just one of her many admirers. But since he is an up and coming star for the school team, she is probably keeping her options open. Thinking quickly, I casually sidle over to her.

"Oh, hi Kim," I say in mock surprise as if I hadn't seen her already standing there.

I can see her roll her eyes at her cheerleader friends. Even so, I am her stupid, little brother's best friend, so she grants me permission to speak by giving me 'the look' placing her hand on her hip and cocking her head to the side. I have to admit, she really is pretty. And her friends aren't bad to look at either. She and her whole posse surrounding me is like a dream come true for a guy like me. But I know this attention won't last long and I am only being acknowledged because of my friendship with Mark.

I've heard that saying, "beauty is only skin deep," but in this case I am thinking, so is intelligence. "Mark mentioned something about him helping you with your science project. But I know someone even better who could help you if you wanted a *really* good grade."

Instead of answering "Who?" like a normal person would, she just raises her eyebrows. I take that as permission to continue.

"That kid, Humphrey Dempsey." I enlighten her as to who Humphrey is by shifting my eyes to him. I don't want to draw Todd's attention by pointing. "He is a high honor student, you know."

"You don't want Mark to help me so you guys can hang out and play your little games?" Her friends laugh and agree with her with their usual elbow nudging and bobbing of heads like chickens in a henhouse.

I pretend to laugh too. "You've got me there, Kim. But Humphrey really is smart. And I know how important it is for you to keep your grades up." I know from Mark that her grades have gone down in science and that in order to stay on the cheer squad she has to get at least a B on her project.

I look over at Humphrey and Kim follows my cue. Without saying a word, she dismisses me by slamming her locker shut and walking away. Like a deer in the headlights, Todd freezes as Kim approaches him and snatches the tattered book out of his grasp. She sees that it is some sort of science book, turns around, and thrusts it into a shocked Humphrey's hands.

"Here," she says "You're going to help me with my science project," and turning to face Todd she adds, "and you are going to leave him alone." With another flip of her hair she turns and struts off, never doubting that Humphrey and Todd will do as she has ordered without question.

A surprised Todd watches mesmerized until she disappears down the crowded hallway. Then he turns his attention back to the hopeless nerd in front of him and snorts. "Ah, we were just messing with you." With that, he and his buddy amble off, most likely to find someone else to pick on.

Humphrey is checking out the damages on his precious book as I approach.

"They nearly ruined it," he mutters sadly. "And now I have to help Kim with her science project? I know what that means. It means that I will end up doing the whole thing for her."

"Oh Humphrey, I really feel for you, man." I shake my head in fake sympathy. "Not only do you have to do your own homework, but now you have to help Kim with hers. I guess that means that she will have to be spending a lot of time with you, and Todd will have to leave you alone, and she will have to spend time with you, and Todd will have to leave you alone, and she will have to spend time with you…"

I can see by the smile forming on his face that he is finally comprehending what I am getting at.

I pat him on the back. "Make the best of your situation and don't blow it."

I am very proud of myself for having done my good deed for the day.

———

"Man, thanks for getting me off the hook with Kim," says Mark with great relief. "She isn't exactly brain surgeon material. She might know all about fashion, hair spray, and makeup, but she thinks texting LOL, OMG, and BRB is the correct way to spell words."

"No problem, I was happy to help you out. I wonder if Humphrey is making the best of a bad situation. Well, speak of the devil, here he is now."

"Hey Humphrey, how is it going?" I inquire.

"Okay, I suppose," he answers as he shifts the bundle of books in his hands.

Just then Todd passes by with his goon squad without even looking our way. Apparently Todd realizes that it is in his best interest to not harass the guy helping Kim with her homework.

"Have you figured out what project you two are going to be working on?" I am a little curious to find out the details, but before he can answer I cut him off.

"Hey, maybe you could demonstrate the effectiveness of suntan lotion. You could have Kim and her friends put on their bikinis and then you could rub the lotion on each one. You know, just to ensure that each one has the same amount of lotion on."

"Oh, gross!" cries Mark before Humphrey can speak. "You are talking about my sister, remember."

I can see that I'm making Humphrey a little uncomfortable too but I continue anyway. This guy could use a little excitement in his dull life. Besides, he is always so serious, maybe I can get a smile out of him. "You could have them lay out in the sun for different lengths of time. Then when the timer goes off you take a giant spatula and flip them over like pancakes."

"Yeah," Mark adds. "And each one would be darker and darker and Kim would come out of it looking like an over-cooked baked potato!"

Mark burst out laughing at the thought and Humphrey even has to smile as he realizes how silly it sounds.

Becoming serious again, Humphrey explains, "Actually what I was thinking of was a demonstration of chromatography."

"Chroma-what?" asks Mark.

"Chromatography. I was going to have her draw a straight line on a piece of white paper…"

"Well hopefully she can at least do that," jokes Mark, who can't pass up the opportunity to make fun of his sister.

Humphrey ignores the comment. "Then she would place the paper on end in a pan of fingernail polish remover. The paper should act as a wick and draw the solvent up the paper by capillary action. Once it reaches the ink it should start leaving bands of different colors as it moves to the top of the paper."

Both Mark and I just stare at him. I have no idea what he is talking about. This Humphrey guy is even smarter than I thought. Not only did he come up with a good science project, but he is also doing something that Kim can relate to. One day, years from now, Humphrey will be rich and famous, and Kim and her friends will be sorry that they weren't nicer to him in high school.

"Well, catch you later Humphrey. Good luck on your projects." I sure wasn't going to ask him what his own science project was about, because he would probably end up telling me and he would lose me after the first sentence and then I would end up looking as dumb as Kim.

Chapter Eleven

So far I am still in the running for the video game competition. The eliminations have been brutal. Not only do you need good hand-eye coordination to play in this tournament, but you need to be able to think fast and make intelligent decisions, all within the given time limit. That is what separates the weak players from the strong. I have to admit that I'm getting pretty good at these games now. I've been able to keep a fairly level head and not panic in stressful situations.

Today is the final game of the competition and I can't wait! Mark is supposed to come and watch me play it. Too bad Becki can't come and watch too. I think she would be impressed.

Oh good, here's Mark now.

Greetings Number 49215. Today's assignment is to travel to the far side of the galaxy where you will join a squad of mercenaries on a rescue mission.

Corporation Security has received a distress signal from the silent alarm of a secret research lab built on an abandoned moon. The moon, once rich for mining, has been stripped bare of all minerals. In the tunnels of this vacant shell, a laboratory was built far from prying eyes. Your mission is to lead your mercenaries there to determine if security has indeed been breached. You are also to determine the nature of any threat and rescue Professor Stevens and his daughter, Lisa.

You will have six mercenaries under your command. All of you are wearing the military version of the Model 4XT battle suit.

I like futuristic stuff, but I'm a little nervous. Unlike historical games where I can make use of my knowledge on the subject, futuristic games are full of surprises and I am as blind as the next guy.

I'm in.

As Mark watches, the game starts. I am in the cargo bay of some kind of transport. Standing across from me are my fellow mercenaries. They are all sleeping or in suspended animation inside their battle suits. I am wearing the same type of suit as the rest of my squad and there are ghost icons on the clear face shield of my helmet.

A row of small colored lights begin flashing on the wall above my troops as well as on the chests of their suits. They are starting to stir as each one awakens from their induced sleep. Lines and tubes are popping off of their suits and retracting into receptacles in the wall with hissing sounds of released air. As my men come to life, they step away from the wall. I step forward too and call out, "Mercenaries, fall in!"

They line up at attention and I walk along reading their nameplates. The first is a dark-haired man with a mustache named York. The second one startles me, for in place of a human face there are robotic circuit boards and wiring covered by a clear shield. A droid. This nameplate reads Y-100.

The next soldier for hire is a very pretty, dark-skinned young woman with jet black hair and large brown eyes. This is Cromwell. For some reason she is glaring at me with resentment. Hmm, I hope I don't have any trouble with this one. She doesn't seem too friendly. Whether in real life or in games, girls are just too hard to figure out sometimes.

Next to Cromwell is another droid called C-200. But it's the next man who surprises me. His nameplate says Badger. I look up expecting to see the greasy, black hair and shifty eyes of the thief from the other game. Instead I see blond hair, blue eyes, and a friendly smile.

"Do you think it's the same Badger?" asks Mark.

"I don't know. He looks different, but it could still be him. The only thing is, this is a single player mission, so these characters are computer generated. I'm not playing against real people this time but who is to say that the computer didn't give me this Badger just to mess with my head?"

"You better be careful, dude."

I continue on to the last mercenary, another droid with B-300 on its nameplate. Oh, I see now. York, Cromwell, and Badger must be their handlers and the initials of their droids are the same as their names: Y-100 for York, C-200 for Cromwell, and B-300 for Badger.

A door slides opens with a hiss and I say real gung-ho like, "Let's get this party started, it's time to earn your pay!"

They follow me out the door and fan out forming a 360 degree defensive circle. They all have a weapon drawn, ready for action. I see the ghost image for my pulse cannon and click on it with the cursor. The pulse cannon deploys by unfolding from the pack on my back and up and over my right shoulder. A small, red sight reticle appears on my helmet window. All I need to do is put the sight on a target and fire. I see that Badger has his pulse cannon ready too.

A quick look at the tracker on my left wrist confirms that our destination, a cave in the side of a large rock formation is just ahead. I relay my instructions. "Badger, take point, Cromwell on me, York, bring up the rear." Only now do I realize the similarity between this time and that time in Kreator's lair. Oh well, if this really is Badger the thief, then having him in front is a good thing. He will most likely locate any traps or ambushes before anyone else. And if he doesn't, well, it is better to sacrifice his life rather than mine. On top of that, I really don't want him to be behind me with his pulse cannon deployed. The old Badger couldn't be trusted. Can this one?

As we get closer to the cave, I see footprints in the moon dust, indicating that many boots have recently come through this way.

Badger stops and sends his droid forward to scout.

I'm a little disappointed that I don't have a droid too. You are only given one life in these games but having a droid gives you an additional one. Should your robot be destroyed, you still have your character's life. This means that I will have to be extra careful.

Badger reports over the radio. "There are two humanoids just inside the cave entrance. I do not have a visual on them but B-300 detects them with his thermal imaging. I don't think they have spotted us."

We need to get past them so I have to make a decision fast. The clock is ticking. "Badger, send in your droid."

There is only silence from Badger's end.

I repeat my order again.

More silence.

Before I can decide what to do, Badger's voice finally comes back over the radio. "Threat removed. We're all clear."

Dare I trust him? We have no choice but to move ahead. Just inside the cave entrance are the remains of the two humanoids. One man's head is smashed in like a crushed melon, and the other is lying in a pool of his own blood. Mental note to self: Beware of Badger as well as his droid. Both can be equally as deadly.

One thing bothering me is that these two dead men don't appear to have been armed. Plus they have the Corporation's markings on their suits and helmets.

Were they really a threat to us, or were they simply friendlies waiting to be rescued? Well, I guess now we will never know. I hate having to rely on Badger to do the right thing, because the truth is I am not convinced if he is truly on our side or whether he is like the Badger of the past and is just looking out for himself like he did before.

Our squad moves further down into the man-made tunnel until we come to an airlock. The airlock is set in a steel wall which seals the atmosphere into the underground complex. We only have room to pass through two at a time so I order C-200 and B-300 to enter first. Cromwell and Badger can handle their droids from out here while York and his droid stay back to cover our rear.

The two droids are transmitting the interior view to their handlers. "The room is a mess," reports Cromwell. "It appears that either somebody has trashed the place looking for something or there was a battle in there."

Badger and Cromwell prepare to enter next. The airlock door shuts behind them and almost immediately Cromwell radios back. "There is a problem! C-200 is down!"

As I enter, I see that C-200 is on the ground with its head bashed in. Whatever did that was very strong and must have caught C-200 completely unaware, but there is no one in sight.

I can't help but wonder if Badger had anything to do with this. Did he order his droid to destroy Cromwell's? For now I have to rely on him, but things are starting to look suspiciously like Badger is up to his old tricks.

Now I have to be wary of him as well as deal with the real enemy.

When York and Y-100 enter through the airlock, we start moving again in the same formation until the passageway opens up into a huge cavern. There is a lot of abandoned mining equipment scattered about. Smaller tunnels are branching off of this one but I decide to take the far one which appears to be larger and is possibly a main route.

Making our way around the piles of rock and slag heaps, we keep our eyes open and sensors on as we search for signs of life. I can hear a distant humming noise becoming louder and gradually sounding closer and I look all around me but see nothing. The humming is very loud now and I can tell it is some sort of motor or engine. I don't even see it until it is directly over our heads; the massive bucket of a giant crane. Hot molten metal is dripping down the sides of it, hitting the ground with glowing orange sizzles. The bucket starts to swing and tip crazily, spilling blobs of its deadly liquid, and we dodge around trying to avoid being hit and burned. Some of it splashes on Badger and he screams in pain but he keeps on running.

There is nowhere to hide. Suddenly the bucket starts to tilt and we all scatter. Only Y-100, York's droid, is caught in the red hot liquid metal pouring from above. Immediately his armor starts to melt, releasing a shower of sparks and wisps of smoke as its circuit boards are fried and melted.

I quickly search for the operator of the crane with the sight reticle of my pulse cannon but I can see no one. The crane starts to move again and we all scatter like ants at a picnic. The bucket is now empty but I still run from it. It's a good thing I do because as it hovers over Cromwell it is unexpectedly released, dropping like a ton of bricks.

"Cromwell!" I yell.

To my relief she steps around from behind it and through the cloud of dust caused by its impact. It must have just missed her by inches. She aims at the crane motor with her pulse cannon and opens fire. The energy pulse hits it and nearly knocks it from its mount. York and I join in until it is ripped from its mounting and is sent crashing against the cavern wall. Even though the control cabin appears to be empty I fire a round at it anyway. It crumples like a tin can and sends a shower of glass slivers raining down.

A pile of what I thought was scrap metal in front of me starts to move and before I can take a step, a mechanical claw grips my ankle. As it rises it grows larger and larger until finally it forms into a giant metal spider-like creature. One of its legs still has me firmly by the ankle while another starts to wrap around my body. Another of its legs is wielding a drill and the spinning drill bit is about to bore a hole into my head. I am thinking this is the end for me until I realize that my sight reticle is aiming directly at the center of the beast. I close my eyes and fire, hoping for the best. The blast tears a huge hole in its core but because it still has a grip on my ankle, the jolt yanks me off my feet and I land hard on my back.

"There are more of them!" yells York.

I shake free of the now limp claw and spring to my feet.

Pouring out of every side tunnel is a huge mass of giant, angry, mechanical arachnids. We all blast away at them, our pulse beams smashing them like insects in a bug zapper.

We make a run for the far tunnel, cutting a path through the monsters with our cannons. Since York is last I yell for him to drop an EMP grenade.

He activates the grenade just as we enter the opening so we are protected from most of the electromagnetic pulse created by the blast. Fortunately for us, that grenade proved to be just the insecticide I had hoped for. Anything back there controlled by a computer is now brain dead. Only a few spiders have survived but we are able to easily finish them off.

In the distance there is the sound of another motor starting up. It's getting louder and therefore, closer. We can hear the sound of heavy tank-like tracks crushing rocks beneath the metallic links as it moves towards us.

We all turn and run away from the sound but when we come around a bend we aren't able to go any further. A cave in of rocks and dirt has blocked us from continuing.

We have to turn back the way we came and confront whatever is in our path. Bearing down on us is a giant boring machine mounted on tracks. A huge spinning drill bit is just about all we can see coming in our direction. I assume this is the machine used for creating this underground maze. This boring machine is heavy duty and made to go through just about anything.

Our shots are simply bouncing off of the massive spinning drill.

"Badger, you'll have to send in B-300," I say. I hate to use the last droid we have but we are out of options.

I can see that Badger doesn't like having to sacrifice his droid. Will he do it? If he doesn't then we are probably all doomed. After some hesitation he reluctantly nods in agreement. The rest of us fall back while Badger and B-300 stay behind.

He sends the droid forward to try to squeeze past the spinning drill. It almost makes it until getting snagged by the drill and is pulled down beneath the right track, where most of its robotic body is smashed beneath the massive weight. The mangled droid is still managing to hang onto the turning track, and as the boring machine crawls on, what is left of B-300 rides the track up and leaps off onto the back deck, pulling itself along until it reaches the control cabin where a humanoid sits at the controls. B-300 takes him out with a shot to the back of the head. Climbing up into the control cabin, it then applies the manual override to make the boring machine veer off its intended course making room for the rest of us to pass through. Unfortunately the droid is no longer able to walk so we have to go on without it.

I check my guidance system and see that if we backtrack a bit we can take a side corridor to our objective.

There is only the injured Badger, Cromwell, myself, and York left. We are getting so close to the end now that I need to keep a really close eye on Badger just in case he tries to pull something sneaky.

We finally come across the right tunnel when Badger gives the signal to stop. Someone is coming! We activate our spiked wrist bayonets which extend out about a foot and a half past our knuckles.

Stepping into view are four armed escorts wearing the rival corporation's uniforms, along with a young woman in a lab coat.

Before they have a chance to react, our four spikes impale and kill the men. The unarmed woman drops her clipboard and jumps back against the wall. She is sweet looking and very attractive as females in games usually are. She looks like a frightened helpless rabbit surrounded by a pack of hungry wolves. I collapse my spike blade back into the sheath on my wrist and ask, "Are you Lisa Stevens?"

She looks confused for a moment before she recovers enough to answer, "Yes, yes I am Lisa Stevens. Have you come to rescue me?"

"Yes," I say with relief. "Where is your father?"

"My father? He is in the lab."

Badger leads the way once again and I stick close to Lisa so I can protect her. We are getting close to the lab now. "Lisa, how many of those guys are in the lab with your father?" We have to be prepared for a fight.

Before she can answer I catch a furtive movement at my side. I can't believe it! I only hesitate for a second before I drop back a step and ram my bayonet into the back of Lisa's neck and out her mouth. Blood splashes my face shield blinding me. By the time I wipe the blood away Cromwell is standing over Lisa's dead body with a smirk on her face.

"That wasn't Lisa!" I scream.

"I know," answers Cromwell calmly as she reaches down to pull a knife out of Lisa's still twitching hand. She tosses it to me. It was mine. I had seen Lisa lift it off of my belt right before I had spotted the rival corporation's logo tattoo on her neck. But if Cromwell saw it too then why hadn't she warned me?

"Come on. Let's get this done," calls Cromwell, running ahead to reach the lab.

Before I can process what just happened, I am off running to catch up to the others. York and Cromwell are ready to go charging into the lab with guns blazing. Well, why not? I draw my gun and we line up outside the door.

Badger kicks in the door and we burst inside. Hopefully we will have an advantage by surprising them. Badger's cannon shot smashes in the chest of one guy and the force flings what is left of him across a table.

One of them attacks me, punching and kicking at me until I am able to drive my bayonet into his eye socket and through his brain. One after another, we fight them off until finally all is clear.

The professor is crouched down under a desk and when he stands up I can see that his body had been covering a young girl.

"You must be Lisa," I exclaim.

"Ya think?" asks Cromwell sarcastically.

Wow, I wonder what her problem is.

As I bend over to help Lisa up I hear two shots of cannon fire. I push the professor and his daughter back under the desk and turn to face more of the enemy. Just in time I see the flash of a bayonet coming straight at my face. I throw myself to one side trying to avoid the blade, which is what saves me. The spike punches through my faceplate, passing right by my eye and embeds itself in my helmet.

I can't believe this! It's Cromwell. Cromwell tried to kill me! I see York and Badger lying dead on the floor from her cannon shots. And now she is trying to take me out. She is glaring at me and I know she's not finished with me yet. We both think of our wrist stingers at the same time, but I grab her hand and wrench it away from me, bring my stinger up and hold the point to her chest.

Tears spring to her eyes as she looks at me pleadingly. "Please," she whispers. "Please don't kill me." Is she contemplating her fate, wondering if I have the guts to do it? Or is she just trying to buy time until she figures out how to get herself out of this situation? I guess we will never know. I suddenly have the urge to do something I would never have the nerve to do in real life; I want to lean over and kiss her, but there is no control button for that, so I finish her off with a shot right through her traitorous heart.

"GAME OVER!"

I set down my controller and stretch my stiff fingers.

"That was some game. I wish my grandma could buy me that one," Mark exclaims.

"Yeah, that sure was intense," I agree. "There I was worrying about Badger the whole time when the one I needed to worry about turns out to be a hot girl."

"Ha-ha, yep. But you wasted her, dude. I wonder if she was a hot girl in real life too. Hey Stu, with a girlfriend like that you wouldn't have to worry about Todd picking on you anymore," Mark laughs.

I laugh too and launch a pillow at his head.

Looking back at the screen, I wonder how I did. Thinking back, it was almost impossible to win, let alone survive. I just hope that I earned enough points to keep me in first place. Ah, here it is.

> Congratulations! You have successfully completed your assignment. As the sole survivor, you are awarded all of the bounty for this mission. The professor and his daughter are now safe and have been returned to their home. Points will be tallied and the winners for First, Second, and Third place prizes will be notified by email. Thank you for participating.

"What the heck," complains Mark. "I want to know if you won now!"

"Well so do I but I have to wait for the email because I don't know how to get in touch with them. When I tried to contact them in the past I got notification saying my message could not be delivered. I wonder what the prizes are? I doubt if they're giving away real gold coins but money would be nice."

Mark shakes his head. "So you don't know when they are going to send the email or how to get a hold of them; you don't even know who 'they' are, and you don't know what the prizes are?"

Gee, when he says it out loud, I feel kind of dumb for sending them money. I don't want to think about it so I decide just to ignore his question.

I guess Mark can tell that I'm a little upset because he adds, "I still think it was pretty awesome."

I have a feeling that he really was trying to make me feel bad, but I think it was probably because he is a little envious so I let it go. "I will let you know how I did in the tournament as soon as I hear something buddy."

Chapter Twelve

Here it is, Monday, and I haven't heard from the game people yet. This waiting is going to drive me crazy. I sure hope I'll find a message from them when I get home.

It looks like Mark is running late for the bus again. If he isn't here today maybe I can build up the nerve to sit next to Becki, or at least talk to her without sounding like a moron. Every day it's the same thing. I see her on the bus and in class, but I just can't think of what to say to her. Whenever I do speak to her, I end up saying something dumb. I wonder if she likes me anyway. I know she saw the Humphrey, Todd, and Kim incident the other day. I wonder if she thinks I'm a hero now. Nah, I doubt it. I wish I knew what she was thinking though. Or, maybe I'm better off *not* knowing. If she thinks I'm a loser then that is something I don't want to know.

Here comes the bus, and here comes Mark, just in the nick of time. "Hey Mark; I didn't think you were going to make it. Was Kim hogging the bathroom again?"

He rolls his eyes. "How did you guess?"

I spot Becki sitting alone in the back of the bus again but as usual, I plop down next to Mark.

"Maybe you should shave her head while she is sleeping and hide her makeup and phone, then she wouldn't have any reason to spend all morning in the bathroom."

"Ha!" he laughs. "Thanks for the idea. Kim's rich friend, Toni, has a car and picks her up every morning, but now my dad says that if Kim makes me miss the bus, they will have to give me a ride to school. That would embarrass the heck out of her. I just might make her do it sometime. I'll take my time and miss the bus and when they have to drive me to school I'll hang my head out the car window with my tongue hanging out like a dog. Then I'll start barking and jumping all over the seats and for good measure I'll even lick the other girls' faces."

"That would teach her! I bet she would never make you late for school again."

"Yep," adds Mark. "And if she did, her friends would probably make us both walk."

"Why on earth does Todd even like her?" I wonder out loud. "She's not very nice to him." Maybe Mark knows something I don't.

"Man, if Todd only knew what she looks like first thing in the morning: eyes crusted half shut, drool running out of the corner of her mouth, breath like a zombie's dirty socks, hairy legs like a Sasquatch, and her hair looks like a three-year-old baby has been dragging her around the house by it."

We both crack up about that one.

I wonder what Becki looks like in the morning. She is probably perfect from the moment she wakes up. Her hair would be all neatly brushed right from the pillow and she's so pretty that she wouldn't need to wear any makeup. Her beautiful blue eyes would be bright and shining and her breath would be sweet.

Mark brings me back to reality as he starts telling me about his last game.

"It started off okay. I blew away a couple of levels of zombies gaining valuable experience points, and I found extra weapons and ammunition. But then I goofed up when I was taking some ammo off a dead soldier zombie and the freak bit me. That was my last life so now I am dead and I have to start all over again. I'll never make that mistake again. From now on I am going to make double sure they're dead."

I sneak a peek back at Becki. She is sitting next to Jennifer Harper. Poor Jennifer doesn't have many friends either. She has what my mom would call a hygiene problem. Well, that's a nice way to put it but it's not quite accurate. The truth is, even though her clothes look like they came from the thrift store, they still appear to be clean. Her hair looks clean too although her face always has a bad case of acne. The problem is that no matter how clean she looks, she still smells bad. I don't know what that girl eats but whatever it is, it sure must not agree with her. Her body is always emitting invisible clouds of odd smells so the other kids usually try to avoid sitting near her.

The great thing about Becki is that she isn't being nice to Jennifer just because a lot of her own friends have turned away from her. Becki has always been nice to everyone, no matter what. She is beautiful inside and out.

I sneak another peek back only this time she catches me looking and smiles. Immediately I turn red and face the front of the bus again. I'm such an idiot! I was so embarrassed to be caught looking at her, I didn't even smile back!

The bus makes its last stop on the route to let Derik and his buddy Josh on. Here we go again. I wonder what insult they are going to throw at me today. Whatever it is, I hope Becki doesn't hear.

I don't believe it. The creeps walked right past without even acknowledging me. They sit down in the row behind us, across the aisle from each other. Derik has to have seen me. So why isn't he saying anything?

The bus starts moving with a jolt and as the driver shifts gears it accelerates like an air force rocket sled. I swear our bus must have a Jaguar 12 cylinder engine in it. It is a bit ironic that for all the regulations and safety rules of the road, school buses seem to be exempt. Our driver speeds through the school zones, and rarely even comes close to a proper stop at red lights and stop signs. And you can forget about trying to do last minute school assignments or reading a book on the ride because you have to spend the whole time trying to keep your balance since there are no seatbelts. I swear that we sometimes take corners on two wheels. We gave our driver the nickname "Otto" because he reminds us of the crazy bus driver from the TV show The Simpsons.

There's the school and Derik still hasn't bothered me. We will be getting off first and then the bus will drop off him and the others at the junior high across the road.

Otto brings the bus to a sharp stop and the door flies open. I can picture him as the jump master in a C-130 aircraft yelling at the paratroopers to "Get out! Get out now!" and pushing them out with a shove of his big, booted foot. Some of the kids have sprung to their feet and are shuffling toward the door like the said paratroopers. I was too slow so now I have to wait for a break in the line of kids before I can get up. Here comes Jennifer with Becki right behind her.

Now I know why Derik has left me alone this morning. He has his bullying sights set on Jennifer.

"Dang," he says loudly. "What's that smell? Did somebody roll in a pile of garbage? Oh, wait. That's not trash, that's just Smellifer. Hey, Smellifer," he calls to Jennifer. "Could you do us all a favor and hang your butt out the window next time?"

Josh laughs. "Ha ha ha. That's a good one Derik."

"Smell ya later, Smellifer," teases Josh.

Jennifer shuffles by with her head down.

Becki pauses next to Derik and says, "Don't be so mean. Why don't you pick on somebody your own size?"

Derik smirks and then casually reaches out to knock Becki's books out of her arms. They fall to the floor with a thud. Jennifer keeps right on walking unaware of what is going on behind her. As Becki bends over to pick them up, Josh kicks them down the aisle and the two bullies burst out laughing.

Without even thinking about the consequences, I jump to my feet, glaring and baring my teeth just inches from Derik's face. "Knock it off, jerk! Leave her alone," I growl.

Derik is so shocked that he doesn't react but I know that won't last long, so I hurriedly go over to help Becki pick up her books. I crouch down to retrieve a notebook from under a seat. There are drawings and writing on the front cover but something in particular catches my eye. A drawing of a girl who looks a lot like…It is! There is her name scrawled underneath the sketch. Moonbeam! Was Becki Moonbeam, the Fairy Princess of Matterhorn?

Becki is standing with hand extended waiting for me to give her the notebook and my eyes go to her necklace with the silver quarter moon charm hanging from it. Does that necklace mean something? Is it maybe a symbol for Moonbeam?

I hand her the notebook and am rewarded with a pretty smile and a polite, "Thank you."

Stepping off the bus, I consider catching up with Becki and asking her about Moonbeam but I chicken out. Mark slaps me on my back. "Man, that was something! You sure surprised that jerk, Derik. To tell you the truth, you surprised me too."

I shake my head in amused disbelief. "Believe me, Mark, no one was more surprised than I was." I have a bad feeling that Derik will tell Todd and then they will both make me pay for it. But for Becki, I would do it again no matter what. At least if I stick close to Mark, maybe it won't be too bad. Kim is not my sister but as long as Todd likes her, and as long as I hang around her little brother, I am fairly safe.

———————

There is one more basketball practice today after school before they make the final cuts. I will be so glad when this is all over with. The only good thing about it is that I won't have to take the bus home with Derik.

I imagine Todd will no doubt see to it that I don't make the team. Actually, that is what I am hoping for. At least Dad can't say I didn't try.

As usual, we run laps and practice endless drills. It doesn't matter what the sport is, basketball, football, or soccer, the outcome is always the same. My muscles ache, I end up with some type of injury and I have to suffer verbal abuse from the jocks who are better at sports than me. Not to mention how my self-esteem takes a beating. If we were competing at video games I would come out on top every time, but unfortunately skills in that area aren't taken seriously and they don't matter, especially to my dad.

It seems like Todd was a little extra rough on me today. His elbow to my face split my lip, and then he has the nerve to get mad at me for it because it caused him to foul. But the good thing was that at least it got me benched and out of practice for a while. Probably the only reason the coach didn't ignore the abuse like he usually does is because this time he drew blood. The star player's fouls are usually overlooked at practice as long as there are no visible injuries. But there is no way to turn a blind eye to blood dripping down someone's face. Man, if I would have realized all of this sooner, I would have tried to catch the ball with my face during every game.

Tomorrow the list of chosen players will be posted on the hallway bulletin board. It is funny how in this age of instantaneous transfer of electronic information they still use an old fashioned bulletin board to relay information. I guess it is a good ego booster for those who have made the cut. But maybe they don't think about how it affects the students who were found to be not good enough. I'm still hoping that my name will not be on it. In this case, I will gladly suffer the humiliation of everyone seeing that I was unable to make that list.

Chapter Thirteen

"Hi Mom, what's for dinner?"

"We are having spaghetti."

"Great! I'm starving."

"And company," she adds

I hope it isn't one of Dad's army buddies again. Normally I don't mind company, but these guys are as bad as him when it comes to judging me and what is going on in my life. Some of them have sons or daughters following in their military footsteps. They brag about how their kids are excelling in school and sports and how they have joined or are thinking about joining the military as well. Dad has to just sit there trying to smile like he is happy for them, when all the while he is probably thinking of how disappointed he is in his own son.

"Please, go clean your room before they get here."

"All right." On my way out of the kitchen I ask over my shoulder, "So who is coming over anyway?"

"I've invited the Everest family over for dinner. It seems the least I can do. I can't imagine it is easy for them to have family meals in their situation."

What? Becki is coming over here? From what I understand, Mom and some of the other ladies from church have taken it upon themselves to help out friends and neighbors who have fallen on hard times. Since they don't want to offend those they are trying to help, they do it in more subtle ways such as inviting them over for dinner and cookouts and passing on clothes that kids have grown out of. Even though I knew Becki's family was having hard times, I never imagined she would ever be coming here.

Normally when Mom says for me to clean my room I move a few things around which to her does not look like an effort at all. Now I *really* have to clean it. But Becki won't even see it will she? Why should she be seeing my room?

It is possible I suppose. What if Mom takes Mrs. Everest on a tour of the house like she sometimes does with guests, and Becki goes along, and they end up in my room, and my mom says, "What's this mess under your bed?" and she pulls out my dirty socks and underwear? Geez, I can't let Becki see that! And what about my airplane models and comic books? Will she think I am a baby for having that stuff? And my superhero poster. That will definitely have to come down. Oh man, I wish I would have known about this sooner.

I hear Dad greeting Mom. "Hello, Buttercup." He has always called her that as long as I can remember. I hope he doesn't do it when the Everests are here. That would be too embarrassing.

———————

Dinner was very awkward. Becki barely looked at me and I avoided looking directly at her. We certainly couldn't talk to each other during the meal with both sets of parents listening. I can just imagine them teasing us about what a cute couple we would make and her six-year-old little brother chanting the old grade school rhyme: "Stuart and Becki, sitting in a tree, k-i-s-s-i-n-g."

Finally with everyone finished with dessert and the dishes cleaned up, the adults prepare to move to the living room.

Mom pauses to say, "Stuart, dear. Why don't you take Michael and Becki to your room? You can show Michael your airplane models."

Show him my airplane models? Why did she have to say that in front of Becki? Why didn't she just go ahead and tell us to run along to my room and play with my toys? It makes it sound like Michael and I are the same age and have a lot in common.

It was more of an order rather than a suggestion, probably because our parents want to talk about things they don't want us kids to hear, or they want us to keep Michael occupied so he doesn't bother them. I guess its okay with them if he bothers us.

"Come on, I'll show you my room," I say with as much enthusiasm as I would have used if I had said that I was going to go cut the grass. Michael is right on my heels, eager to see what wonders might be hidden behind my door, while Becki follows meekly behind.

"This is my room," is all I can think of to say. Becki and Michael just stand there looking over the layout and contents. While Michael eyes my airplane models with excitement, I notice that Becki is looking uncomfortable and ill at ease. I pull the chair out from the desk and offer it to her. Mom is always telling me to act like a gentleman so I guess she would be proud. Becki smiles and says, "No thank you, I'm fine."

Michael impulsively goes for the airplane model displayed on my desk. It is a Ju-87 Stuka with the 37 mm cannon under the wings; my favorite. I automatically move to snatch it up it before he can grab it and possibly break something on it. Only too late do I realize that was a dumb move to make in front of Becki.

"Oh, here, let me show you this," I say, handing it to him and trying to act like I don't care whether he breaks it or not.

"Be careful with it, Michael," she warns.

"This is a Stuka," I start to tell him, but he has already lost interest and is snooping around the room with my precious model in his grubby little hand.

"He has liked airplanes ever since he was a baby."

He's still a baby, I am thinking, and he is making me nervous running around and touching everything.

The hyperactive boy makes a couple of circuits around the room and then brings my plane in for a rough landing on my desktop. There is a cracking sound that makes my heart jump and the tail wheel breaks off.

"Oh Michael, now see what you have done! You better put that down and tell Stuart you are sorry."

"Ah, don't worry about it. He can keep it if he likes." I have to be cool about this and can't carry on like a little kid, even though I am fighting the urge to grab the plane out of his hands to check for further damage and to repair the broken wheel.

"Why thank you, Stuart." She smiles at me, showing the dimple in her right cheek and looks directly into my eyes. "What do you say, Michael? Tell Stuart thank you."

Michael is already airborne again, making airplane noises as he circles the room. "Errrrr! Thank you, Stuart. Errrrr!"

We watch him for a minute and then without thinking, I sit down on the edge of my bed. It suddenly occurs to me that I am in an awkward situation. Should I stand back up because she is still standing? Offer her the chair again? But she already said no to that. What do I do? Thankfully Becki decides for me and she sits down next to me.

"You have a nice room, Stuart," she says politely. "I miss my bedroom. It's nice to have a place of your own to get away from everything."

"Oh, don't you have one in your new place?"

She shakes her head sadly. "No. We had to move into a tent and our camper at the campgrounds. Didn't you know?"

Those words hit me harder than Todd ever could. Even if he had slammed me flat on my back and knocked the wind out of me I would not have been as surprised. My Becki living in a tent? I knew they had moved to the campground but I thought they were living in one of the rental cabins there. I had no idea that they were actually living in a tent. What do I say to that?

"No, I didn't know that. I'm really sorry, Becki. I wish there was something I could do."

In an attempt to lighten the mood, she jokingly elbows me in the ribs, smiles reassuringly, and says, "We're fine, Stuart. Really, it's not so bad.

"Anyway," she continues, "I wanted to thank you for sticking up for me on the bus this morning."

"No problem," I say smiling back at her. "Derik was being his usual jerky self and I just got tired of it. Some people shouldn't even be allowed out in public. Besides, he shouldn't go around picking on girls."

"Well thank you for that, it means a lot." And then casually, and without looking at me, she puts her hand in mine and lightly squeezes it.

My heart is beating so fast and I know my palm must be sweaty, but I manage to squeeze her hand back. She turns her head to look deeply into my eyes, and just when I am getting up the nerve to try to kiss her, she crosses her eyes and sticks out her tongue comically before giggling and jumping to her feet. "So what do you want to do?"

I grin up at her. My heart is now completely hers. "I don't know. Do you want to play a video game?"

Her face lights up as she answers enthusiastically, "Sure! I would love to. What games do you have?"

Michael, who I had completely forgotten was in the room, chimes in, "Oh, boy! Video games. Do you have Wi-Fi?"

Chapter Fourteen

Come on Mark, where are you? If he doesn't get here soon, he's going to miss the bus. I have decided not to tell him all of the details of Becki's visit, but I do have news for him. I wish he would hurry up. Oh good, finally! "You guys really need a second bathroom," I call out as Mark runs up.

"I almost didn't make it today. Kim's face broke out in huge zits last night and she had a major meltdown when my mom told her she had to go to school today anyway. Unfortunately, she chose the bathroom to have her fit in."

"Oh, wow. It kinda serves her right though for always making fun of Jennifer."

"That's what I say," he agrees.

I couldn't hold it in any longer. "Guess what, Mark? I won!"

"Won what? The video game competition? You actually won it?"

"Yep, I can't believe it but I won first place!"

"Weren't you supposed to get a prize? What did you get?"

"I don't know yet," I admit. "That's the weird part. I had to send them the name and address of a tailor shop so they can take my measurements. But I don't know what they are supposed to measure me for."

"That does sound weird. Hey, maybe they are going to send you a suit of armor or some chainmail. Wouldn't that be cool? Oh, there's the bus."

As I climb up the steps of Otto's C-130, my mind is occupied thinking of what my prize might be. Maybe it's some kind of cool costume. Maybe even from one of the games I have played.

When I see Becki smile at me and wave from the back of the bus, I wonder if she would be happy for my winning. When I mentioned the game contest to her when she was over, she didn't seem too interested in talking about it. It's kind of strange because she really liked playing the video games with me at my house. And when I had started to ask her about Moonbeam she changed the subject. Well if she really was Moonbeam, maybe she is upset about being killed off and not being able to advance. I just dropped the subject then because I didn't want her to feel bad and think I was just bragging.

Mark and I talked about my possible winnings all the way to school. My good luck continued when Derik and Josh didn't get on the bus at their stop. Now if only my name isn't on the basketball team list, this will be a perfect day.

———

"I'm home Mom!"

"Hi Honey. How was school today?"

"Great! I didn't make the team. I mean…"

Mom laughs. "I know what you mean. The important thing is that you tried."

"So, Mom. Did you make an appointment with the tailor shop yet?"

"Well, you know Stuart, I am very busy."

At my look of disappointment she laughs. "Yes, of course I made the appointment. In fact we should probably leave right now. I'll put dinner on when we get back."

We hop into her little, cherry red car and we are off. Mom likes her car and I think that it suits her just fine, even though it doesn't look like a typical mom car. It fits her bright and cheery personality. To be honest, I don't even know what model or make it is, because the only thing we have ever called it is "Mom's little red car." I like it too. Sometimes when we are cruising at a breathtaking 30 mph we will put the windows down and crank the radio up. Some guys are embarrassed to be seen with their moms, but not me. I actually enjoy going places with mine. She's fun to be around.

The tailor has a shop in the strip mall about ten minutes from our house. A little bell tinkles over the door as we enter. A small Asian guy comes out from the back room and gives Mom a friendly greeting. His name is Mr. Song and he looks like he is at least a hundred years old. Dad says that he came to America when Vietnam fell to the Communists. Not only is Mr. Song my dad's tailor, but he also gets a lot of business from the military. Mr. Song's work at tailoring dress uniforms is flawless as far as the military is concerned, and every patch and ribbon that he sews on a uniform is guaranteed to pass the most critical inspection.

I remember Dad telling the story of Mr. Song ranting to some new military customers that not only was his work guaranteed, but if their commanding officer ever had a problem with it they should come see him and tell him to his face. Now that I see how small and fragile looking this guy is, I can see the humor in the story. Little Mr. Song waving his bony finger in the face of someone two or three times his size, chattering away in broken English about how he is going to chew out their officer if need be to defend his work. Of course, Mr. Song's work is legendary, as are the custom unit patches that he and his daughter make by hand, so it would behoove any officer who wished to make use of his establishment and expertise to not question him.

"Hello, Mr. Song. We have an appointment to get my son's measurements."

"Yes, Missy Maxwell. Very good."

A big smile breaks out on Mr. Song's face. Mom has that effect on people. I have to admit she is pretty for a mom but she also seems to radiate a happiness that is contagious. People can't help but to feel good around her. Sometimes I wish it would work on my dad's mood more.

"I take care of you boy, Stuart. You sit. Sit."

Leading me into a curtained fitting room, he asks, "Stuart, what hand you write with?"

I hold up my right hand wondering what that has to do with anything and he busily starts measuring my arm from elbow to wrist. Then he measures the width and length of my hand, four fingers and thumb.

He writes his findings down and announces, "Okay, we done."

I follow him out and look at Mom with a puzzled expression. She must have read the look of confusion on my face, plus she could hear what was going on behind the curtain so she knows this was not the usual taking of measurements for clothing. "Are you sure that is all you need Mr. Song?"

If it had been anybody else he probably would have been offended that his judgment or ability was being questioned. But this was Missy Maxwell, so he just smiles and nods repeatedly. "We done, Missy Maxwell. We done."

She accepts his assurance and they exchange bows of mutual respect. I call out, "Thanks, Mr. Song." I can't wait to talk to Mom about this once we are outside.

"Mom, all he did was measure my arm and hand. Even I know that he needs to do more than that."

"Well you still don't know what he was measuring you for. What were you expecting? Did you think they were going to fit you out in a tuxedo so you could take your best girl to some fancy video game awards ceremony?"

I give her a sheepish grin. "Aw Mom, you are my best girl."

She laughs and says, "Oh, honey, you are such a liar, but I love you for it."

I laugh too. It's nice to be able to joke around with her. I sure can't do much of that with my dad.

"Oh, I know!" she continues. "Maybe you were expecting Mr. Song to make you a superhero's costume, with a cape, mask, and cute, little tights."

I give her my most serious face. "You won't be joking around about it when you are kidnapped by an evil villain and you need me to rescue you." I run over to the car like I'm flying and jump into a superhero pose with feet apart and hands on my hips.

"You're a strange kid."

"And you're a strange kid's mommy," I joke.

"Get in the car before somebody sees you," she giggles.

She starts the car and begins to back out of her parking spot when all of a sudden somebody lays on their horn behind us causing Mom to slam on the breaks. "I swear there was no one behind us when I started backing up!"

"I know, Mom. I saw it. They just came racing up behind you."

She is embarrassed, for she prides herself on being a safe driver. I can hear a man yelling and swearing, and I crane my neck around to get a better look. There is a large black SUV with fancy wheels and tinted windows still sitting behind us blocking us in. Mom looks scared and ready to cry. With one last obscene gesture directed at us out his open window, the SUV races away with a squeal of its tires.

"I'm sorry," Mom calls out as they drive away.

"What a stupid jerk! You didn't even do anything wrong," I say trying to make her feel better. Boy, this is one time I wish my dad was here.

Chapter Fifteen

Poor Mark was really upset at the bus stop this morning. Ever since his sister Kim had her face break out with huge pimples a few days ago, she has been miserable and is making everyone in that house share in her misery. One would think it was the end of the world the way she has been acting. A visit to the doctor found what the problem was but not the cure. Kim had an allergic reaction to something that caused her face to break out with nasty red bumps so she has to go through a series of allergy tests where the doctor has to prick her skin with about a hundred needles to find out what she is allergic to.

Now suddenly her "friends" have deserted her and have told her some lame reason why they can't drive her to school anymore, and even Todd, who worshipped her, is giving her the cold shoulder. He usually follows her around trying to get her attention, but not anymore. Even though I'm kind of glad that Kim is getting an idea of how hurtful she has been to others in the past, I can't help but feel a little sorry for her now. Still, it's not right that Mark has to suffer too.

And Mark isn't the only one who is suffering because of this. Now that Todd doesn't like Kim anymore, my friendship with her brother doesn't give me any protection at all. Todd is finding every opportunity he can to make me miserable. I avoid him the best that I can but there is always gym class, and I dread that as much as Kim dreads finding a new zit in the morning.

———

Entering the kitchen after school I spot a package addressed to me on the table. It's here! I pick up the box and shake it. Whatever it is, it isn't that big or heavy. Could it be a new game, or maybe a t-shirt and gift certificate? Going into my room and closing the door, I sit down at my desk and carefully open the package. What is this?

It looks like a long-sleeved glove, but there is only one here instead of a pair. I slide it on and examine it closely. It fits me like a glove, as the saying goes, no doubt thanks to Mr. Song's precise measurements. I notice some metallic threads woven into the leather-like material that look like some kind of leads or sensors. Reading the instructions, I discover that the glove is actually a new high-tech video game controller. With the glove on, I don't need any type of joystick, or controller or anything else. The glove is supposed to sense what I am doing and respond depending on how I move my hand and arm.

Following the instructions, I log on to the site listed for a practice session. Not sure what to expect, I rise to my feet and back up a couple of steps. On the screen appears a large muscle-bound Viking, armed with an ax and shield. Reaching down to my side, I pretend to draw my sword. As if by magic, it appears on the screen. Putting my hand by my side, I can only see the end of my blade, but when I lunge forward with my arm outstretched, I see my arm and the whole sword grasped in my hand thrusting toward the Viking. He starts to advance on me and the battle begins.

I raise my gloved hand and strike downward and sure enough, my sword arcs down onto the Viking's shield. I swing my hand across his midsection and my blade slices through the air right where I had aimed.

The Viking swings his ax at me and I counter with my sword by reflex, successfully blocking his hit.

This is so cool! I decide to get creative and see what all it can do. I make a motion like I am tossing the sword up in the air and catching it by its blade and then pretend to throw it at the Viking like a spear. It actually worked! The glove duplicated on the screen exactly what I had done with my hand. I don't know if it was luck or skill but my blade split the Viking's head in two, splattering brains and blood everywhere.

Totally excited now, I pull off the glove and call Mark.

Mark doesn't waste any time coming over. He was probably glad to get out of the house and away from Kim's drama.

As soon as he arrives I start another game so I can show him how it works. This time the game has me flying a high performance futuristic fighter plane. I close my fist like I am actually gripping the plane's control stick. I turn my aircraft and bring my weapons to bear by turning my wrist and then use my thumb to push the imaginary fire button. Thumb pressed to the left for missiles or to the right for machineguns. After I blow a couple of the enemy out of the sky, I let Mark give it a try.

Mark and I are about the same size so the glove fits him pretty good. He is about to start when the words, "New player?" flashes on the screen. Wow, how did it know someone different was wearing the glove? Did it read our fingerprints? We type out Mark's name and the game begins.

This game has him armed with a semi-automatic pistol pitting him against flesh-eating zombies. I couldn't have picked a better game for him.

The first zombie is a slow walker, so Mark has time to get used to the unfamiliar glove. He raises his hand and aims at the undead monster on the screen. He pulls the imaginary trigger but nothing happens. I wonder if maybe the game only works for me. I can see the gun in his hand on the screen but why isn't it working?

"Try chambering a round," I suggest. Mark goes through the motions of pulling back the slide and letting it slam forward and we can see the act being duplicated on the screen. This time when he pulls the trigger the gun discharges and blows an arm off of the slow walker.

"All right! That's what I'm talkin' about," he yells in excitement. With that he is off hunting zombies with as much eagerness as a little kid hunting for Easter eggs.

When his magazine goes empty he automatically rams in a fresh one. It seems that the game is gradually becoming harder and more challenging according to Mark's abilities. And if he shows a weakness in something, it presents more of those same types of challenges until he improves enough to move on to something more difficult. This glove is something else. It must be some new prototype and I am the chosen game tester. But I'm not just any game tester; I am a champion game tester!

We take turns playing for as long as possible until I finally just ask if he can eat over. Mom gives her permission and we eat in my room while we take turns learning about the game system by shooting, stabbing, and blowing things up. All in all it has been a very constructive afternoon. It is getting late by the time we finally have to stop. If Mark hadn't had to go home, we probably would have played until dawn.

When I go to thank Mom for letting Mark eat over, I can tell that something is bothering her. She tries to act interested in what I am telling her about my new gaming glove but her thoughts seem to be on something else. I hope that she and Dad aren't fighting. I know they sometimes have their differences, but I don't think they would ever let it come between them permanently. If they did have a disagreement, hopefully they will make up and tomorrow will be better.

Chapter Sixteen

I can't believe my eyes! Not only is Mark at the bus stop in plenty of time, but who should be tagging along at his side but his sister, Kim. I guess it must really be true that her good buddies have dumped her. The poor girl, with no brains and now no good looks, she has no redeeming good qualities to fall back on. She has been reduced to joining the ranks of all of us social outcasts. You would think that she is some new kid that doesn't know anybody the way she is hanging her head and refusing to make eye contact with anyone. Her face is covered in red, angry looking bumps. You can tell she tried to cover them with makeup and she is trying to hide behind her hair but nothing can be done to make them disappear completely. She looks like she has chickenpox or something.

Mark and I start talking about my game system and about how much fun it was yesterday and about future possibilities that the game might offer us. As soon as I get on the bus I can see that Becki is not there in her usual spot. I quickly scan the other seats but she is not here. Where is she? Even as Mark and I talk about other things, I am only half listening. My mind is on Becki and where she might be. Did she miss the bus? Did she have an accident? Is she sick? I hope she's not hurt or sick. Who knows what could have happened to her with living in a tent. I can imagine her catching pneumonia from sleeping in a leaky tent with cold rain water dripping on her all night long. She could be lying on her death bed (or in this case, death sleeping bag), because her family doesn't have insurance and can't afford to take her to the hospital. That would be terrible.

I'll talk to Mom about it after school. She'll know what to do. At least I'll *try* to talk to her since she still seemed preoccupied this morning as though something was bothering her. I guess her and Dad didn't make up yet and she is upset about it. Whatever it is, it's probably Dad's fault and all will be well again when he tells her how sorry he is for whatever he did.

It seems like everybody is having some type of problem lately. No one is really happy because life is throwing a curve ball at everyone at the same time, everyone that is, except Humphrey Dempsey.

Thanks to Humphrey's help with her science project, Kim not only received the highest grade she has ever gotten in science, but she is also doing better in other subjects because Humphrey decided to help her with her other classes too. With her having very little social life these days, she's had plenty of time to spare for schoolwork, plus Kim was grateful to have someone who offered her friendship without judging her for her appearance. Humphrey gave of himself without asking anything of her in return.

Ha! He's not fooling me. Humphrey is getting something in return. The guy is no dummy, and he isn't a shallow person. He can look past the bumps on Kim's face and see the beauty that is still underneath. It doesn't matter to him that her physical looks have changed. All that matters is that he somehow can see the goodness inside of her that hasn't seen the light of day ever since she started hanging around with the snobby, rich girls in school. Now that they haven't been around to influence her, she is becoming more humble and nicer to be around. Yep, by the time Humphrey has finished with her, she will be as beautiful on the inside as she once was on the outside. And one day when her face is back to normal, he just might have a pretty, as well as intelligent friend. Or if he is lucky, maybe even a girlfriend.

When I get home I bring up the subject of Becki to Mom. I am trying to act cool and casual about it but it has been bugging me all day. I think Mom saw through my act but fortunately she didn't tease me about it. She just made a few phone calls and finally found out that Becki's little brother had been sick today so since her mom had to work, Becki had to stay home to take care of him. Little kids get sick a lot, but Mom knows that it's important for Becki not miss too much school for that. She and a couple of the ladies let Mrs. Everest know that one of them would look after Michael anytime he was ill so that Becki wouldn't have to miss class.

I feel better now that I know what is going on. Becki should be back on the bus on Monday then. Maybe I will strike up a conversation or even sit next to her. Well, maybe not. If I sit by her then Mark might make a big deal about it and embarrass me. I guess it's safer just to wave and say hi. I'll have to wait until Mark is not around before I take the next step.

———————

I guess whatever is going on between Mom and Dad is still going on. She still seems upset, and he has a constant angry frown on his face. I sure hope it's not because of me. The only good thing about it is that Dad has way too much on his mind to bother about what I am up to. Usually when he is home he tries to limit my video game playing time and tries to think of tasks and chores for me to do instead. I like it better when he gets really busy with work, or is sent overseas on a mission or something. Then Mom takes over our family life. She is much easier going and less demanding of me and my time.

Dad has been in the military for so long that he doesn't realize he brings it home with him. With him being a colonel, everyone has to obey his every command without question and it must have gone to his head. Now he expects me to stand at attention and salute and say, "Yes, sir, whatever you say sir," and never argue about anything. I'm not saying he doesn't care about me. I know he does. It's just that I don't want to be treated like a soldier. I want to be treated like a son that he isn't ashamed of. It would be nice if he acknowledged and was proud of the things I do well instead of always pointing out my flaws.

I make a beeline for my room to try out my glove again but when I bring up the game site, instead of a game, the computer offers me a fencing lesson. I really wanted to play a game but what the heck, I'll give it a try. I always wanted to learn how to fence anyway. I am instructed to find a short stick to work with so I search my room until I find a ruler in my desk drawer. Maybe this will work.

The instructor on the screen bows introducing himself as Saint-Didier, the father of French fencing. He explains that the French foil consists of a blade, guard, cushion, handle, and pommel. He then demonstrates the proper method of holding it. I grasp the ruler in my hand wondering how long this is going to take. I'm in the mood for shooting zombies or searching mazes for monsters. I get enough lessons in school so when I am at home I just want to have fun.

"No, no. You are holding it wrong. If you hope to survive your duel today against Senor Miro, I would advise you to pay attention to detail." He shows again the correct way to hold it and this time I get a nod of approval. It is a little difficult to take it seriously when he has a sword and I am holding a ruler but I decide to try harder to get it right.

Finally I get permission to put down my stick and pick up my virtual sword. I have completed my first lesson in fencing from some French guy long dead.

Senor Miro and I spar for a while. I'm really getting into it, using some fancy footwork while lunging, thrusting and parrying, until we end in a draw. Well I didn't win the match, but then I didn't lose it either. All in all it was more fun than I thought it would be.

I want Mark to come over and give it a try but he turns the invitation down. I am surprised about that because I know how much he enjoys playing, but what is even more of a surprise is his reason. Kim came home very upset about her ex-friends talking bad about her. She is crying and depressed so Mark wants to stay home and try to cheer her up by having pizza and watching a funny movie with her.

What in the world is going on? I thought they hated each other. They are always acting like the other one is a pain and saying mean things to and about one another. How can you act like you hate someone, yet care enough about them to give up something you enjoy doing just to make them feel better?

That makes me think of Becki, saying what a pest little Michael can be, and then uncomplainingly giving up her after school activities so she can get home to watch him, and staying home from her classes to care for him when he is sick. Being an only child, maybe I am missing something when it comes to siblings. Maybe it would be nice to have a brother or a sister after all.

Chapter Seventeen

Mark and Kim actually make it to the bus stop before I do for once. Kim's face looks a little better but there are still enough of the bumps left to make her feel self-conscious. She actually says hi to me, which she doesn't ordinarily do. And she even thanks me for hooking her up with Humphrey. I think I like this new Kim.

Mark stays by his sister's side so I just join them until the bus comes. Kim gets on first. Guys and girls slide over to the outer edges of their seats so that she isn't able to sit with any of them. As she gets closer to the rear, Becki slides closer to the window to indicate that she will share her seat. Kim smiles gratefully and settles in.

"Kim's having a really hard time," Mark confides to me in a low voice. "As if she's not having a bad enough time with her face breaking out like that, her so-called friends have deserted her, the other cheerleaders want her off the squad, Todd has started picking on her, and her best friend Toni is talking trash about her online."

I know who he is referring to. Toni is the rich girl who has her own brand new car and was giving Kim a ride to school every day. This is the same girl who got a good citizenship award for doing a special project for handicapped kids which they had a big write-up about in the newspaper. She volunteers as a candy striper at the hospital and is the high school cheer captain. But most of the people in these admirable organizations don't know what she is really good at. She is an expert at talking bad about people behind their backs and she stirs up loads of trouble on the social networks. She seems to thrive on the drama and the excitement of posting nasty comments about someone and having her followers back her up with mean comments of their own until they have everyone else turning against her victim too. She spreads rumors and outright lies with the aid of her computer and then sits back waiting for the fireworks to begin with no concern for the person's feelings or how it affects their life.

Now Toni has set her sights on tormenting Kim. Just as Todd's parents would never admit that he and Derik have social problems, Toni's father would never believe that his sweet little girl is a cyber-bully capable of causing so much harm. It seems that the worst bullies are the ones whose parents refuse to believe their kids are picking on others.

After some silence Mark says, "Man, I've had it with Todd. Now that he doesn't like Kim anymore, he is making her life miserable and he is even threatening to beat me up today after school because I said I was going to report him to the principal. Well if he wants to beat me up, he is in for a big surprise."

I don't like the way he said that. What surprise is he talking about?

"What surprise? Did you learn how to fight like Bruce Lee overnight or something?" I joke.

Mark doesn't answer at first but then he looks furtively around and unzips the backpack at his feet. He opens it just enough for me to peek inside. Holy crap! Is that a gun?

I look at him in shocked disbelief. "What the heck are you thinking?"

He quickly closes the pack and smiles. "Shhh, don't say anything. Anyway, it's not what you think."

It's not what I think? I know what I saw! Trying desperately to gather my wits, I know I have to do something. This is serious and would not end well. I can't let my best friend get in trouble for doing something so stupid. Someone could die and nothing would be solved. Somehow I have to convince him not to go through with his plan. But how?

The bus is slowing down for our last stop. Mark's hands are clenching the back of the seat in front of him, bracing for Otto's crash test dummy stop. Now is my chance. I reach down and grab his pack, spring to my feet and am sprinting down the aisle before he can stop me.

Otto snaps the door open to let on more students and I jump down the steps knocking hard into Derik who had just started to take his first step up. He stumbles back into Josh cursing.

"Hey! What the…"

He doesn't get the chance to finish his comment before Mark comes barreling through after me shoving the surprised bully out of the way a second time. Everyone on the bus bursts out laughing at the sight of the red-faced, tough guy standing there with his mouth hanging open. I can hear the laughter behind me and I know that once the shock wears off, Derik will be out for blood. I can't worry about that now though. I have something much more serious on my mind. I can't let Mark catch up to me until I find someplace private to have it out with him.

We run so far that I have a painful stitch in my side but I can still hear Mark a short distance behind me. I don't know where I'm going since I am not familiar with this neighborhood but finally I see a wooded area up ahead on the other side of the street.

Thankfully there is a break in traffic and I shoot across without incident. I can hear tires screeching and horns blaring, as Mark isn't so lucky and he has to slow down to dodge traffic. Entering the woods, I spot a creek and the culvert that leads to it. The perfect spot. I run in splashing through the shallow water and wait for Mark to catch up.

When he finally stumbles in, we are both gasping for breath. "What the heck did you do that for? Are you crazy? How are we going to get to school now? And give me my pack!" he demands between breaths.

He makes a grab for the bag but I block him. "I'll give it to you, but you have to listen to me first."

"Stuart, I told you it's not what—"

"Mark, shut up and listen to me! This is serious. Think about what you are doing. There has to be a better way to handle this. You will end up in jail and someone could get hurt or killed. Think of your family and what this would do to them. You are about to ruin your whole life over someone who isn't even worth it. Come on man, use your head, there has to be another way to—"

"It's not real you idiot!" Mark blurts out cutting my rant short.

"What? What are you talking about?"

"I tried to tell you it's not what you think. It's not real. It's one of those toy guns that shoot plastic pellets. I colored the red end of the barrel with a black magic marker so it would look like the real thing. I didn't really want to hurt anybody; I just wanted to scare Todd. So you see you did all of this for nothing."

"Man, *you* are the idiot! I'm glad you aren't stupid enough to bring a real gun to school, but don't you know you can get in just as much trouble by bringing a fake one? You could be suspended or maybe even arrested! With all of the school shootings lately, these things are taken very seriously."

Mark is starting to look scared. "I guess I wasn't thinking. I figured since it wasn't real, I wouldn't get into trouble for it. I guess you really saved my butt."

"I would do anything for you, Mark. Man, you are like a brother to me." I hold out my fist and he bumps it with his.

"Thanks, bro, I feel the same way," he says. "But now what do we do? We're late for school and we don't have any way to get there on time."

We walk toward the mouth of the tunnel trying to decide what to do when a man steps in front of the opening, blocking our exit. He is a tall, scruffy looking guy squinting at us in an unfriendly way. His t-shirt and jeans are dirty and he has a scraggly beard covering his lower face. We stop, even though we want to run, but there is nowhere to run to. He looks like a homeless guy or a drug addict or something. I don't like this one bit. I would much rather be on that bus facing the wrath of Derik than to be here right now facing this guy.

The bum spits a brown stream of chewing tobacco which lands within inches of our shoes and wipes his mouth on the back of his hand. "Well, well, well, what are you two boys up to? You musta took a wrong turn somewhere to end up on my turf."

"We don't want any trouble, mister," I manage to say. "We were just leaving."

"Now just hold on there a minute," he says, as he spits another stream of juice, this time splattering my pant leg. "Where are you going in such a hurry?" Then he spots Mark's book bag. "What do you have there in that pack?"

We take a nervous step back as he takes one forward. For a moment I think of the fake gun inside and contemplate pulling it out. But what if he has a real gun and he thinks ours is real and he shoots us. No, I decide that would be a dumb thing to do.

When he reaches out to take the backpack I notice a tattoo on his arm that is very familiar to me.

"Were you in the Air Cav, mister?" I ask with genuine curiosity.

"What?" My question catches him off guard and he pulls his hand back.

"I recognize the tattoo on your forearm. That's the First Cavalry Division, isn't it? My dad is in the First Cav. too."

My look of admiration brings a hint of pride to his face and his hard eyes soften a little. He tells us that his name is Sal and he is a veteran who was injured while fighting in Iraq, but when he got home there was nothing left here for him. No wife, home, or job. Nothing but the constant pain left from his injury to keep him company in his loneliness.

According to my dad, I know this story is all too common. So many soldiers have come home from serving their country only to find themselves treated as outcasts instead of the heroes they have shown themselves to be.

"Here," I say, reaching into the bag. I find Mark's lunch and hand it to Sal. "And here, I have some spare change if you need it." I dig into my pocket and come up with a five dollar bill and some coins. I hand it to him and Mark digs around and comes up with some too.

Sal accepts our offerings gratefully. I feel good that we were able to show him the gratitude and admiration that this country failed to honor him with. It isn't until we walk away that we remember our own problem.

After throwing around a couple of ideas, we end up at Mark's house where no one is home for the day. "Now what?" we ask ourselves. It is too late to go to school, and there is no way to get there anyway. Plus, I have no idea where my own backpack is with all of my books. It got left behind on the bus when I took off with Mark's. For all I know Derik might have gotten a hold of it and spilled out the contents scattering all of my books and papers around like the caveman he is. I imagine him crouched down scratching his head in confusion trying to figure out what all those words mean.

Finally deciding that we might as well eat, drink, and be merry, for tomorrow we die, we help ourselves to some snacks and play some of his video games. We watch the time and get out to the bus stop just as it pulls up.

When Kim steps down she hands me my backpack with everything still inside. Boy, am I relieved to get that! "Thanks, Kim. I really didn't expect to see any of my stuff again."

"You can thank Becki. She is the one who picked it up and held on to it all day. She gave it to me after school so I could give it to you."

I wonder what Becki thought when I took off like that. It's too bad I can't tell her about it. I can't tell anyone. Even though the gun wasn't real, Mark would still be in a lot of trouble if anyone found out.

We all part ways and head on home. I have never in my life skipped school before so I have no idea what to expect. I guess I'll pretend like I had a normal day and act cool about it.

I try not to think about it. But even if I had thought about it, I could never have imagined just what all was in store for me and how these next twenty-four hours would change my life forever.

Chapter Eighteen

Uh-oh! That's strange; Dad's car is in the driveway. He usually doesn't get home until later. That can't be good. Although I am not hungry yet, I will go inside and ask Mom what there is for dinner like I always do. Just act casual.

Wait a minute! Holy crap, what happened to Mom's car? The rear taillight is busted and there is a dent on the driver's side door. Geez, look at that, I wonder how that happened? I sure hope she wasn't hurt. I better go inside and find out what's going on.

"Mom, I'm home!" I bellow as the screen door bangs shut behind me. On my way to the kitchen I see my dad out of the corner of my eye standing in the middle of the living room. I can tell he has been pacing and is agitated about something.

"Jeb Stuart!" he calls in his no nonsense parade ground voice. It is both a summons and a warning of impending doom, making my body feel hot and cold at the same time with nervousness.

I enter the room, dropping my pack along the way. I usually leave a trail of items from the front door to my bedroom as if I need it to find my way out again but from the look on Dad's face I am guessing I will never have need of that trail of 'breadcrumbs' again. I don't think I will be leaving my room for a very long time.

"Just where have you been," he demands. It wasn't really a question.

My mouth drops open, but no sound comes out. I glance over at my mom and I can tell that she has been crying. Dad looks about ready to explode. He is clenching his fists at his side, there is a large vein bulging in his forehead and the cords in his neck are straining as though he is working out. I have never seen him this angry before.

His voice booms out again making me jump. "I asked you a question, soldier! Where have you been?" I knew this was the last time he was going to ask.

I look at Mom for a clue as to what is going on. What do they know? How much do they know? Has the school called already? We sure caused a scene jumping off the bus like we did. Maybe somebody told them about that.

I decide to play dumb and let them be the ones to tell me how much they know. "At school," I lie.

"You were at school? Don't you lie to me boy. The school called to find out if you were sick since you weren't in any of your classes today. Now do you want to tell me again that you were in school?" His tightly clenched fists are trembling slightly at his sides. He has never hit me before. Is he about to now?

"No, sir." I take a peek at Mom for help but she isn't looking my way. I'm all on my own.

"We also got a call from a mother of one of the younger boys complaining that you shoved her boy off of the bus. It sounds like you have had a very busy day today; skipping school and picking on kids younger than you are."

What? Picking on kids younger than me? You gotta be joking! Derik is twice my size. He is the one who picks on me and I have never once told on him. This is so unfair. Derik has twisted it all around to make himself look like an innocent victim and me look like the bully. I know I have to explain; but wait, there's more.

"I am very disappointed in you, Stuart. I never expected any of this from you. Do you know your mother was involved in a car accident? It's lucky she wasn't hurt. And then she has to come home and deal with this as well. What if she had been badly injured, and with you nowhere to be found?"

Whoa! If he is trying to make me feel guilty, it's working. What a rotten thing to say to a kid.

"Go to your room, you're grounded!"

I look over at Mom and then back at him. "Don't you even want to hear my side?"

"Do as I say. Go!"

On my way to my room I hear Mom start crying. I feel bad for hurting her and I wish I could go back in there and give her a hug. I would tell her how sorry I am but I can't, not with Dad standing there glowering at me.

I barely get my door closed when I hear the sound of his combat boots stomping up the stairs. I sit on my bed and mentally brace myself for another scolding but he marches in without a word, snatches up my new gaming glove, and walks out with it. I guess I won't be seeing *that* for a while.

I lay miserably on my bed until dinnertime. Our meal is so quiet, I can hear them chewing. Silence at the table is very unusual for us. There was no Dad complaining about work, or the traffic. Mom wasn't talking about her day or what was going on in the neighborhood. And nobody was asking me about school. Oh yeah, I almost forgot, I wasn't *at* school today. The whole evening has been surreal, to say the least.

Not even able to finish my dinner, I excuse myself and go straight to my room where I stay until my alarm wakes me in the morning to get ready for school.

Chapter Nineteen

Thankfully, by the time I get up, Dad has already left for work. I'm glad because I am not ready to face him yet. This will give me a chance to try to make things right with Mom, or at least I can try. I find her in the kitchen making my breakfast.

I follow up my "Good morning, Mom," with a little hug. I think about adding a kiss on her cheek, but I don't want to make it look like I am trying too hard. Acting normal isn't easy when there is so much tension in the air between us.

"Good morning, Stuart," is all she says as she flips some pancakes bubbling on the griddle. I wait, but she doesn't say any more and the silence is killing me. I start tapping my fingers on the table and humming just to fill the quiet room with some noise.

"Are you hungry?" she finally asks.

Good, that is a good sign. At least she is talking to me, even if she hasn't looked at me yet.

"Starving," I fib. Truthfully my stomach is in knots and I don't feel much like eating at all.

"Good," is all I get back from her. Come on Mom, talk to me! I want to ask if she is okay, but then she might say something like, "Of course I'm not okay. My only son has ripped out my heart and stomped it into the ground. I will never be okay again. I no longer have a son; you are dead to me!"

Well maybe that is a bit dramatic, but unless she starts talking to me I don't know what to expect from her at the moment.

"Here you go," she says, placing a stack of pancakes in front of me. "You better hurry so you're not late for school." She kisses me on the top of my head, and turns to leave.

It is now or never. "Are you okay, Mom? You know, I mean, from your accident and all? You weren't hurt or anything?"

"I am fine. I was just shaken up about the whole thing but I wasn't injured so don't you worry."

I know this should make me feel better but it doesn't. There is something else going on that she is keeping from me. I know her well enough to know that she is not telling me everything. It must be me. I'm the one who hurt her and I feel terrible about it. For a brief moment I even wonder if Mom and Dad are about to break up because of me.

I have a lot to think about as I choke down my pancakes and then walk to the bus stop. I think of Mom and how I have disappointed her. And about Mark and all we have been through together; and Becki with her messed up life. I guess compared to hers, my life really isn't so bad. And then there is my dad who I can never seem to please no matter what I do.

He wouldn't even listen to my side of the story; he just goes and takes my controller away. It isn't fair; I worked hard for that controller. It took me hours of playing to hone my skills. It may have seemed like I was just being a lazy couch potato to him, but for me it was a lot of dedication and work. And what about all that time I spent reading up on and watching videos about the latest developments and competitions? Did he think I was just messing around wasting my time? Maybe I wasn't on a ball field, but I put out the maximum effort in order to win that prototype of the latest state of the art controller. And then when I actually win it, instead of congratulating me, he takes it from me. If he is not interested in what I like to do then why can't he just leave me alone and let me enjoy things on my own?

He is always trying to run my life, telling me what I need or don't need. I'm not one of his soldiers; I can think for myself. Over the years, he has tried to push me into activities that *he* thought I should like doing. First it was t-ball, then karate class, then Boy Scouts, and now basketball. Why doesn't he ask me what *I* want to do? I suppose next he will want me to think about joining the Army, so I can be in the Air Cav just like him, and his father before him.

Turning the corner I see my classmates waiting for the bus. Well, at least I didn't miss it.

"Hey, Stuart!" calls Mark. "Hurry up, the bus is coming."

I jog the next half block to the stop. My legs sure do hurt from all of that running I did with Mark yesterday. I slow down and limp the last few steps. I wanted to beat Mark and Kim to the bus stop but I was too distracted this morning so that my timing was off. I am anxious to find out if he got in trouble too but as soon as I see him I know that things must have worked out better for him than they did for me. He looks way too happy.

"Hey guys, how's it going?" I ask unenthusiastically.

"Not bad." Mark answers with a smile. "How is it going with you?"

"Funny you should ask," I respond sarcastically. "I got busted yesterday. The school called my house wanting to know where I was all day long. So now I am grounded and my dad took the game glove away from me. And I have no idea when or if I will be getting it back."

"Oh man, I'm sorry to hear you got busted. I lucked out. The school called my house too but my parents weren't home. Kim answered the phone pretending to be my mom and she told them I was sick but that she had forgotten to call in. It was a pretty good imitation. She gets a lot of practice doing that because my mom has her answer the phone whenever salespeople call. Anyway, she pulled it off with no problem. She even thanked them for calling. It was great!"

Suddenly he frowned, looking worried. "Hey Stu, you didn't tell your folks that you were with me at my house all day, did you?"

I can see that my answer will either make or break his day. If I had told my parents the truth then Mark would be in as much trouble as me, if not more.

"Nah, of course I didn't. I wouldn't rat on my best friend."

A look of relief washed over him. On one hand, I'm glad he didn't get in trouble but on the other hand, I'm a little upset that I am the one who got in trouble while he gets off scot free. After all, it was his poor judgment that got us into that situation in the first place.

I plaster a phony smile on my face and change the subject. "So, did you ever make it to the next level of that game we were playing yesterday?"

"I made it last night, but just barely. I thought I was toast when I fried the gatekeeper's butt with my flamethrower and then all of a sudden all of these zombies started crawling out of the…"

Ah, Mark, my good buddy. I really do care about your quest for the virus antidote in zombie land, but… who is that fair maiden in yonder bus window?

That's about all the Shakespeare I know, if it even is Shakespeare. Does she like Shakespeare? I don't know, but being a girl, she probably does. I would recite it for her if I could, but then if she doesn't like it I would feel like a fool. Oh, what does it matter? The way I ran off the bus yesterday, she probably thinks I'm a big loser anyway.

"Stuart, are you even listening to me?"

"Yeah, sure Mark."

"Then what did I just say?"

Awkward pause.

He follows my gaze as the bus pulls up. "Hah, I knew it! You have Becki on the brain again, don't you? I wonder if I can find the antidote for *that*."

I can feel my face turning red. "What are you talking about, Mark? For your information, I was thinking about all the homework I have to catch up on from yesterday."

"Aha! Now I know you are lying! You don't care enough about your schoolwork to give it any thought during your free time. Besides, even a zombie with his eyes blown out can see that you like Becki."

I didn't think it was that obvious, so...another uncomfortable pause.

"Aw, I'm just giving you a hard time," Mark admits with a laugh. "Seriously though, you should sit with her. *I* might be able to read your mind but *she* can't. If you like her, then you have to let her know you like her."

I was about to deny again that I like her, but I know it won't do any good. The truth is that I do like her a lot and I would give anything to have her for my girlfriend. If I keep saying I don't like her, she might discover what I said and think those are my true feelings.

I climb onto the bus, away from my dad and my own troubles. I'm going to do it! I am going to start letting Becki know how I feel about her, and then maybe, just maybe, I will find out that she feels the same way about me. Maybe.

The bus looks more crowded than usual today. No wait, most of them are just bunching up in front. Jennifer must be passing gas again. That poor girl puts out more gas than Gas Mart. No wonder nobody wants to sit by her.

I walk by the packed front seats of kids laughing and yelling back and forth. A few have their heads bent down, checking their phone messages and texting. They act like whatever they are doing is so important but my guess is, they are probably just texting each other:

"Hi Suzy, what are you doing?"

"Oh nothing, just sitting next to you, what are you doing?"

"I'm sitting next to you too."

"HAHAHA, LOL, ROFL."

Becki is sitting in the dead zone behind Jennifer. And is that an open spot next to Becki? Mark sees it too; he better not sit there. He shoots me a sly grin over his shoulder. Don't you dare, buddy. Good, he is taking the one across the aisle from her.

Now just be cool and don't blow it.

"Hi, is this seat taken?"

Ah, you moron! Now why did you ask her that? Just sit down.

"No, have a seat Stuart. Here, let me make more room for you."

No, please don't move, I want to sit as close as possible to you.

"Thanks." I plop down a little too hard and make her bounce up like we are on one of those inflatable jumping toys.

I can see you smirking, Mark, knock it off!

She smiles at me, showing her cute dimple. "It's so nice out today, the air smells like flowers. Can you smell it?"

I take a deep breath in but all I can smell are bus fumes and the poor girl sitting in front of us.

Becki is looking at me with eyes as blue as the sky. Her hair is long, soft, and sun-kissed blonde. I heard that expression on a TV commercial once, sun-kissed blonde, and I immediately thought of Becki's hair. And she is beautiful on the inside too. Becki can even overlook Jennifer's problems which believe me, are not always easy to overlook.

Answer her quick and quit staring at her!

"Yeah, the flowers smell good."

Say something else you fool, this is your big chance. Ask her if she saw that funny posting on the web. No, YouTube. No, you dork, they don't have internet; she lives in a tent, remember?

The bus is starting to move. "Do you like movies, Becki?" Ugh, what is wrong with me, of course she likes movies. Everyone likes movies.

"Sure, I like them," she answers politely.

"What I mean is; would you want to go sometime? To a movie, I mean, with me?"

Suddenly the bus jerks to a sharp stop, scattering books and other personal items every which way.

I instinctively fling my arm up in front of Becki to keep her from hitting the back of the seat in front of us.

Kids are standing up trying to see what happened. "Hey, Mark, what's going on?"

"I don't know. A black Hummer just cut us off and is blocking the bus...Oh man, it's your dad, Stuart! And he's getting on the bus."

I can feel my face doing a slow burn, turning redder by the second. Dad, don't you know that you are embarrassing me in front of my friends? How can you do this to me, especially in front of Becki?

I can see him through the sea of kids, talking to the bus driver. Maybe this has nothing to do with me. Maybe he is here for some kind of government business. Becki is looking at me with a question in her eyes. I can tell I am as red as a beet; I can feel the waves of heat washing over me and my armpits are wet with sweat. I shrug my shoulders to let her know I don't have a clue what is going on and then I start praying. *Please don't let him come this way. Please, please, please.*

But luck is not with me today. Here he comes.

His voice booms out loudly, causing a hush to fall over the entire busload of rowdy kids. "Stuart, I need you to come with me."

Gosh, Dad, can you say it any louder? Or maybe you think I'm not embarrassed enough already.

"But Dad!"

"Now, Stuart, let's go."

"But what about school?"

Like a blast from a cannon, his voice thunders throughout the bus, "Now!"

Oh my gosh, in front of Becki; how will I ever live this down? And that look he gave me actually scared me. Man, I hate you! How can you do this to me? I'll come with you, but I will never forgive you for this. You have ruined my life.

Everyone is staring at me. *Just walk down the aisle and avoid eye contact with everybody who's snickering and whispering about you.* How can I ever face any of them again?

When we get out to his vehicle, I avoid looking at all of the curious faces in the bus windows.

"Get in," he orders.

I climb into the passenger seat and it isn't until he gets behind the wheel that I notice that he is carrying his gun. He doesn't normally do that. What was he going to do, haul me off at gun point if I didn't cooperate?

"When I tell you to do something, I expect you to do it."

"But why?" I question, unable to keep my voice from trembling. I am determined not to cry. "What is so important that you had to pull me off the bus in front of everyone? They were all laughing at me."

"I do not have to explain myself to you, Stuart, nor do I have the time. As your father, I know what is best for you and someday you will thank me for it, but for now you will respect my decisions and obey me without question."

Man, if you only knew how I really feel about you! That's it, play the tough guy and squeal the tires. Let everyone see what a mean jerk you are.

I suddenly can't help myself; after years of suppressing my true feelings, I can't hold back any longer. "Well in case you haven't noticed, *I* have a mind of my own and can think for myself. Did you ever think that maybe you *don't* know what is best for me? You say you care about what I want but you don't. All you care about is what *you* want for me."

Oh, man, I can't believe I just said that out loud. I must have said those words to him a thousand times in my head, but never out loud. I think I might have gone too far this time. I'm in for it now. His fingers are squeezing the steering wheel, almost like he's tightening them for a punch. Maybe he is getting ready to backhand me or worse yet, pull out that gun and kill me!

"You ran a stop sign," I stupidly point out.

I probably should not have said that either but it seems like now that I have finally let my feelings out, I can't stop.

"Geez, Dad, you almost hit that car! Maybe you should slow down."

Suddenly there is the back end of a police car directly in front of us but instead of slowing down, my dad steps harder on the gas and swerves around in front of it. I look back and see that he is now following us with siren blaring and lights flashing. "Dad, that cop wants you to pull over," I say, even though I know he sees it in the mirror.

This is not good and so not like my dad. Speeding, driving recklessly, running from the cops, and wearing a gun? I wish he would say something. Anything! He is making me really nervous. This silence is becoming unbearable. He always has something wise to say whenever I speak my mind, so I have learned that it's best not to. But now I did it. I bet he wasn't expecting that, but then neither was I. Now what? Gosh, I almost wish he would yell at me. At least that would be something familiar. This whole thing is freaking me out.

Finally he clears his throat. "I'm sorry for pulling you off the bus like that, son."

Finally! Now I can start to breathe again.

"I know what it's like to be your age, and how important it is to be accepted by your friends."

I doubt it.

"The last thing a kid would want is for their old man to make a scene by pulling them off of the school bus in front of everyone."

Okay, now this is getting even weirder. He never refers to himself as the 'old man' nor does he allow me to.

"But I have too much on my mind to worry about that right now," he continues, "and I can't explain everything to you because I am still trying to process it all myself."

I don't understand what he is talking about. Where is he taking me? To my surprise the police car, with lights still flashing, passes us and Dad accelerates to keep on its tail. I don't understand. It looks like we now have a police escort. There is the army base up ahead. Why would he be bringing me here instead of to school?

Can this day get any stranger? Maybe I am dreaming and I will wake up any second to my messy room and the smell of Mom making breakfast.

We usually have to show our military IDs to the soldiers guarding the gate, but this time even though their guns are drawn they wave us right through and the police car is left behind at the gate. What is going on here? There are armed soldiers swarming everywhere. Sirens are blasting and there are several fire trucks and ambulances. That van there looks like it is all shot up with bullet holes and the area around one of the buildings is roped off. I am craning my neck from one side to the other trying to take it all in. What the heck is going on?

Dad slams on the brakes and throws the Hummer in park. "Okay, Stuart. Listen to me very carefully. We are going inside and I want you to follow me and stay close."

I have never been in this building before and I wonder what it is. Geez, all of the windows are busted out and the broken glass is scattered everywhere. "Dad," I say in a low voice. "What happened to this place? It looks like a bomb went off here."

"Sorry, Colonel Maxwell, I can't allow him to come in here, sir."

The pimply faced young soldier nervously choking the life out of his rifle doesn't look much older than me.

Dad tightens his jaw and narrows his eyes giving the soldier his sternest look. "I don't have the time or the patience to argue with you, Private. Now get out of our way or so help me…"

Boy, I bet that soldier wishes he had a change of pants handy. Suddenly, I am glad that my dad is so intimidating. I am starting to get excited about what we are doing here and I would have been disappointed to have been turned away now.

We step inside and I feel like my eyes are popping out of my head trying to take it all in at once. This outer room looks like any other office, except for what looks like bullet holes in the far wall. And what is that stain; is that blood?

We continue into the next room. Wow! It really does look like a bomb went off in here. I can still smell the smoke, and there are flash or powder burns on the walls and floor. Many of the computer monitors are blackened and busted. Some of the ceiling panels are missing too. Even I know it would take something big to do this much damage.

Wait a minute, is that more blood? Did somebody die in here? Maybe this isn't so cool after all. I sure hope nobody notices how much I am sweating. Actually, I hope nobody notices me at all because if they do I might be made to leave.

One man, who looks to be about Dad's age, is standing in the middle of the room with a clipboard in his hand. Being the army brat that I am, I could tell a person's rank before I could read. He is the sergeant major, and is the man who really runs the show for my dad. "Colonel, what is he doing here? You can't bring a kid in here."

Dad brushes off his comment with, "You let me worry about that. Is everything ready?"

"I won't be held responsible for this," the sergeant major sputters indignantly. "And I am not babysitting."

"I asked you if everything is ready!"

The sergeant major gives in under Dad's steely stare. "Yes, sir. Everything is ready to go."

A young female soldier, with short spiky pigtails sticking straight out from each side of her head, speaks up from her position in front of a computer terminal. "Sir, we have made contact again."

"Which monitor?"

Over there, sir," she points and pops her gum loudly.

Snatching up a microphone my dad speaks loudly into it. "Styx, this is Rolling Stones, over."

A voice comes over the static charged speakers, along with an image on the monitor screen. "Rolling Stones, this is Styx," it says. "Where have you been, man? The concert has started, and we can't get tickets."

Between the code names and the special language they are using, I am trying to make sense of their conversation. From what I can see on the screen though, that guy doesn't look too good. Is that blood, or camouflage paint on his face?

Holy cow! I can hear the sound of gunfire in the background and then a different soldier appears on the monitor.

"I'm sorry, Buttercup. I'm afraid I won't be able to join you guys for the party."

Dad's code name is Buttercup? That is what he calls Mom. Oh gross, that guy is coughing and hacking up blood!

"Don't you say that," Dad tells him earnestly. "Don't even think it. I know how much you enjoy a good party. Hang tough, Cricket."

"Tell my wife I love her, will you, Buttercup?"

"Don't talk like that, Cricket. You can tell her yourself when you see her. I got the party van all fixed and ready to go. We'll swing by and pick you up. You just hang on, Cricket, and that's an order. Hang on!"

If I didn't know any better, I would think my dad is about to cry.

They lose the signal and everyone works frantically to try to get it back. I don't understand everything that was said but my guess is that something bad happened to some fellow soldiers and my dad is in charge of rescuing them.

"Alright son, listen carefully to what I am about to tell you. You probably figured out for yourself that a bomb did go off in here, set off by unidentified terrorists posing as minimum wage migrant workers, and it couldn't have happened at a worse time. Somewhere out there, I am not at liberty to say where; some of our Rangers were on an important mission. A helicopter from my unit was on its way to pick them up, but in the process of doing so they came under fire. The chopper was damaged and some mighty fine men were badly wounded. They think they can still take off and pick up the stranded men but the enemy anti-aircraft gun that took them down is still in the area, so they would be shot down as soon as they left the ground. There is no one else in that vicinity to help them. Even if we sent someone, help would most likely arrive too late and they would not be able to destroy the enemy gun because of where it is positioned. The only hope we have of rescuing our men is a remote control drone which is controlled by this equipment."

A wave of his hand makes it pretty clear to me that I am standing in the wreckage that had once been the drone's control room. At any other time, being in this room full of high tech computers and equipment would have been a dream come true for a kid like me, but from the look of things, it doesn't seem to be a very safe place at the moment. Instinct tells me I really need to focus on what is being said.

Dad pauses to allow me to take it all in. This is a lot to absorb into my brain. What with the bomb damage, drone warfare, and secret Ranger mission, it has all of the drama and excitement of a Hollywood action movie.

After a moment to allow me to process everything, he continues, "When we lost contact with the drone, it automatically switched to autopilot, just as it is programmed to do. Due to the bomb damage you see around you, and a serious Chinese military computer virus that we have been dealing with, gaining control of the drone will be very tricky. Now, I need to briefly explain the workings of our drone to you."

"I have flown drones in my games plenty of times. Is it anything like that?" I ask.

"Well, Stuart, it is similar, but I want to make one thing very clear. What we have here is not a game. Human lives hang in the balance which makes this very serious. Now let me fill you in quickly while they are trying to restore communications.

"The drone in question here is called Venom. As you probably know, drones do not carry any humans on board so they are often used when a mission is too dangerous to risk a manned aircraft. Venom does have a crew, only its crew controls it from safely on the ground. In this case, it is controlled from here in this room. This drone is equipped with a camera in its nose from which our ground pilot can see what he would actually be seeing if he were there in the craft."

He then proceeds to show me a diagram of the positions of the downed chopper, the enemy anti-aircraft gun lying in wait, as well as the position of the soldiers of whom the chopper was on the way to pick up before it was disabled. This is awesome! This is so much like my video games that I don't have any trouble understanding it but I can't help but wonder why my dad is telling me all of this.

"Sir, isn't this information classified?" the sergeant major asks disapprovingly. Then he shakes his head and mutters, "Why is this kid even here?" I don't know if he meant for my dad to hear that or not, but I guess he did hear it.

"I know what I am doing," Dad snaps. "My son knows that what I am telling him is not to be repeated. Besides, without his help we may not be able to carry through with this rescue. Like it or not Sergeant major, 'this kid' may be our last hope."

I can't believe he just said that about me, his loser son.

As if what my dad said gives me the proper clearance like I am some high paid civilian contractor, I stand up straighter. "What do you need me to do Dad, er, Colonel?"

"Okay, Stuart," my Dad continues, "this is our dilemma. As I said before, the drone has to be controlled from here."

Looking around at the damage I don't see how that will be possible given the damaged state the control room is in.

A soldier steps away from one of the least damaged computers. "It's ready, Colonel."

Now I see what he has been over there working on. "Is that my game glove? What on earth did they do to it? They ruined it!"

My one of a kind, state of the art, gaming glove has wires sprouting out all over it. I feel like I could cry, but Dad is talking to me again and I have to focus.

"Being as the drone's controls were destroyed in the blast, we thought that we were helpless. Fortunately for us, I still had your controller in my briefcase. The techs have wired it up to what is left here of the drone's control station. As I said earlier, the drone is at this very moment circling on autopilot. Once we take it off autopilot, well, we can't say for sure what will happen. Regardless, we have to try. This may be our one and only chance. You are here strictly as a consultant, since you are the only one familiar with how your glove works. Captain Rockwell here will be controlling the drone."

Captain Rockwell, the man Dad is referring to, is dressed in civilian clothes and is sitting next to the pigtail girl with his back to me. He is wearing one of those wide brimmed, blue cavalry hats as favored by the troopers of General Custer's Seventh Cavalry. He swivels slowly around in his chair and looks me up and down like he would at something disgusting that was smeared on a bathroom wall. "I don't need the kid's help," he says arrogantly. "I can fly this baby in my sleep."

Dad bangs his fist on the table, making me and several others jump. "Now I am going to say this only once, Captain, so listen carefully. Those are my men as well as my friends in danger out there so I will not tolerate anyone or anything that might hinder their rescue. My son knows more about this controller than anyone else in this room, including you, and the only reason I am tolerating your presence here is because this is your job. So with that being said, should he offer you any advice about operating Venom that has to do with this controller, I advise you to listen carefully to him and follow his direction or I will kick your rear end so hard I'll be scraping the mud off my boots with your teeth! Do I make myself clear?"

Pause.

"Yes, Colonel."

Way to go Dad! I feel like cheering but I play it cool.

"Lieutenant Hughes, please brief my son on the workings of the drone."

"Yes, sir."

This man, whom I decide that I like much better than that Captain Rockwell, wins me over with his friendly smile, which is as large as the smiling, bright yellow SpongeBob clock on the wall. "Our drone is a SVD-2, a new prototype that is to replace the old RQ-1 Predator. Like the Predator, it looks like a small airplane with a turbofan engine in the rear. It too is launched by radio control from an airfield in the area where it will operate. Once the ground crew has it in the air, we take over and control it at long range by linking through a satellite, much like the internet. We are the ones who fly it and have full control as to where it will go and what it will do. If we lose contact with the drone, the GPS satellite navigation takes over and it will circle in a preset orbit until we gain control of it again, or if it is programmed to, it will simply fly home. We can control a drone anywhere in the world from right here," he says as he points to the floor for emphasis. "Or at least we could have, before all of this happened."

"Preparing to switch to manual control," one of the techs announces.

I see Captain Rockwell writing down some final calculations when something occurs to me. "Dad," I blurt out. "He's left-handed."

"Is there a problem with that Stuart?"

"Heck yeah, there is a big problem with it. The glove was made specifically for a right-handed person. But that is not the only problem. It was also tailored to my measurements for a custom fit. The glove won't fit him exactly right and so the sensors might not respond accurately. And someone who is left-handed is probably not as precise and coordinated with their right side as they are with their left."

Captain Rockwell begins pulling the glove onto his right hand with some difficulty so a couple of technicians hurry over to assist him. It is a tight fit but they manage to get him into it. "Don't you worry about it, sonny," says Rockwell over his shoulder. "I know what I'm doing."

It's too late to do anything about it now. The glove is on and the drone has been switched over to manual control. It is all up to Captain Rockwell from here on out.

I step up behind him to get a good view of the screen. "Careful, Captain Rockwell, just let it level out for now, then you can make small adjustments until you see how it responds to you." I sure hope he will listen to me. "This glove is extremely sensitive to any slight movement. Even so much as a muscle twitch causes it to anticipate what your next move will be. It takes time to get used to it."

"Do as he says Rockwell. Steady. Keep it steady."

You tell him, Dad.

"Alright," says Rockwell. "I think I have the feel of it."

"Arming missiles," announces Pigtails. Her name is Specialist Truman but I can't help but think of her as Pigtails because of her hairstyle that looks so out of place in this environment. "Sir, it appears one of the missiles has malfunctioned and we only have one in working order."

"Well, we better make that one count then," says Rockwell, a little too sure of himself. "I'm taking her down now. Here comes the Cavalry to the rescue!"

He dips his hand and Venom responds a little too sharply. He tries to correct it by tipping his hand up slightly and the drone bounces a couple of times but then levels off.

He is flying it a little rough. I don't think he is as ready as he thinks he is. I have to say something.

"Captain Rockwell, the controller is designed to pick up impulses from muscle flexing as well as merely the tilting of your hand. Be very careful or you will over-compensate."

"I got it kid, no sweat."

He is trying to act calm and in control but I can see that he *is* sweating and so am I.

"Colonel, satellite imaging has spotted the gun's location," says the sergeant major. "It is located inside the mouth of a cave. In order to reach it he will have to come in at a heading of 3-5-0, but then once he clears the mountain, he will have to drop down to get a visual."

"Roger that," answers Rockwell.

Lieutenant Hughes steps in beside me to enlighten me as to what is going on. "Once Specialist Truman, gets a visual on the target, she will 'paint it' with the laser mounted on the drone. The Hellfire missile will hone in on that spot and if the blast doesn't get 'em then that hundred pound log traveling at over Mach 1 will."

I can see that Rockwell is having a little difficulty keeping the drone smooth and steady using the ill-fitting unfamiliar glove, but he seems determined not to admit defeat. "We're going in, boys."

"SAM!" someone yells. "Enemy SA-7 launched! Take evasive action!"

"Launching flares," calls out Pigtails. "Jammers on."

Captain Rockwell swears under his breath. There is nothing to be seen on his monitor now except a blue screen. I then realize that the blue is the sky. "What happened?" I ask Hughes.

"Someone on the ground launched a shoulder-fired SA-7 surface to air missile, or in other words a SAM, at the drone. Thanks to Specialist Truman's quick reaction of activating the flares and electronic jammers, the SAM could not get a lock on Venom, however as Captain Rockwell was trying to dodge it, he may have been a little too quick on the controller. That move broke the data link from the satellite to the drone. Whenever that happens, the drone goes back to circling on autopilot. Once the captain gains control of it again, he will give it another try."

There was a lack of confidence in the way this was said that made me think that maybe Hughes wasn't so sure that Rockwell could pull this off. That was just too close. He over compensated, just like I knew he would, and that shoulder-fired missile was almost the end of Venom. Even I can see that this is never going to work with him flying it.

"Dad, let me try it."

Rockwell immediately speaks up. "I got this Colonel."

"Dad, listen to me. There is only one way in there. Remember the stories you told me of flying NAP of the earth?" *Yes, I was actually listening to your old war stories.* "Remember how you said that you flew your helicopter below the tree tops or up and down over them like a rollercoaster? That is the only way this drone will get down in those valleys for a clear shot. I've done that kind of maneuver hundreds of times in my games."

Good, so far he hasn't said no. Does that mean he is actually considering it? Everybody in the room is staring at me in wide-eyed disbelief.

"Permission to restore contact," says Rockwell.

"Negative," Dad tells him.

A speaker starts beeping and all of the computers seize up and freeze at the same time.

"There it goes again," yells Pigtails. "That darn virus is locking up the whole system."

"Come on people, tell me somebody has a handle on this," pleads Dad hopefully.

"I got nothing, Colonel," says one of the techs.

"Me neither," says Pigtails, shaking her head.

"Hughes? Anything?"

"I'm working on it, Colonel," he says as he starts banging away on the keyboard faster than a teenage girl texting the latest gossip. He hits "enter" and then pauses to see if it works.

Everyone holds their breath in anticipation.

Nothing happens.

Whatever this virus is, it is interfering with all of their computers.

"Dad, I have an idea but I need a laptop. Do you have yours with you?"

"Yes, I do." Without even asking any questions he leaves the room and comes back seconds later with his computer. "Now what is this about, Stuart?"

"If I understand correctly, you are using a link through satellites to control the drone but somebody is obviously blocking that link. My thought is; what if you established and used a different link?"

"What are you saying son? Do you know of another link that we can hook up to?"

When I see all eyes are fixed on me, my confidence wavers and I wonder if I can pull this off. Then Dad powers up his laptop and looks at me for further information. The confidence in me that I see in his expression gives me the boost I need. I know computers. I can do this.

Without hesitation I tell him to type in CyberDan. com.

He quickly types it in and is taken to the website.

"Log in as 49215. The password is bEcki109." I am a little embarrassed to have to announce that password to the room. I see Pigtails smile when she hears it but other than that nobody makes fun of me.

Dad surprises me by saying, "This is the site where you won your glove, isn't it?"

I wonder how he knew that. "Yes, sir. I am thinking that if you can utilize their computer, which seems to be extremely advanced, we can possibly control the drone through it. The glove was developed to work specifically with their computer so there is a good chance that it could work."

To my amazement, the sergeant major speaks up in support of my idea.

"The kid may be on to something, Colonel. Do you remember what happened back in Grenada in '83, when those Rangers were pinned down in that house? The Cubans had them outmanned and outgunned. The Rangers had lost their radio communication and were unable to call for help. One of them found that the civilian landline in the house was still working, so he used his calling card to make a long distance call back up to their home base at Fort Benning, Georgia. Fort Benning then relayed the information back down to Grenada and in-theater air support saved them from the Cubans. Maybe a landline is exactly what we need, sir."

Dad isn't saying anything, but he is listening, and thinking.

Then Rockwell says what is on all of our minds. "How do we know if we will have their cooperation, or if it will even work?"

Lieutenant Hughes answers him with, "I think that as soon as they realize we are who we say we are, and they can see what the drone is seeing, they will cooperate." He takes over the laptop and starts typing. "As to whether it will work or not, unless you have a better suggestion, I would say it is well worth a try."

"Lieutenant Hughes," I say. "One of the games that I played on this site involved my piloting a drone."

"Thanks Stuart that might be helpful." He hits more keys and then waits. While he is waiting for a response from the website he asks me, "I need to know how this glove was used. Was it through a desktop computer or a laptop?"

"I have only used it with the desktop computer that we have at home, though I sometimes hooked up our flat screen TV to use as the monitor."

Lieutenant Hughes, deep in thought, finally comes to a decision and nods his head. "In that case I would suggest the techs restore the glove to its original condition as quickly as possible, sir. We may have need of it."

With the wave of his hand Dad signals for two technicians to retrieve the glove from Captain Rockwell. They scurry over to their workbench with it, where they hover over it like elves in Santa's workshop, tinkering and working their magic with their tiny tools.

"I'm in!" Hughes shouts in excitement. He begins typing away faster and faster. The room is filled with the sound of the clickity, clack, clack, of the keyboard. He is either typing in code, establishing links, or exchanging social status information with some cutie at the computer company. But, whatever he is doing, he is definitely good at it and knows his stuff.

At just about the same time the glove is ready, Hughes has the site ready to go.

"Dad, I know I can fly Venom if you just give me the chance."

He thinks hard for a moment and then makes his decision. "Rockwell, please relinquish control to my son. Besides being the only one here who is familiar with and has experience in using the glove, he has a steady hand and his hand-eye coordination is outstanding. Right now he is our best, if not our only, chance."

What? Did I hear him correctly?

"Sir, you can't be serious!" Rockwell exclaims in disbelief. I guess he can't believe that a mere kid is about to take over a job that he has been trained for and does on a regular basis. "That's a five million dollar plane!"

"Rockwell, my mind is made up. The lives of those stranded soldiers are of more importance to me than what that plane is worth."

"But he's just a kid. Alright! But you are taking full responsibility for this." He jumps up angrily, shoving his chair back so hard it almost tips over, and starts pacing on the far side of the room.

Gee, he sure changed his mind in a hurry. I wonder if it was the murderous expression on Dad's face, the "don't you dare argue with me" tone of his voice, or the fact that my dad subconsciously placed his hand on his holster as he spoke.

I'm suddenly experiencing a sensation I am unfamiliar with when it comes to my dad. I am proud of him.

I slide my hand into my glove and it feels good, like a part of me that has been missing has been restored. Now to get down to business. Man, if I blow this… no, I can't even think like that. There is far too much at stake here. I can't think about the reality of what I am about to do. I have to think of it as though it was just a game otherwise my nerves might get the better of me. It's just a game. A game I must win. I can do this. I *will* do this.

"Whatever you do Stuart, do not touch this red knob on the control panel," instructs Pigtails. "That is the self-destruct button. We would only use that to blow up the drone in extreme cases in order to keep it from falling into enemy hands."

"Yes Pi…" Oh my gosh, I almost called her Pigtails! I have been thinking of her by that name since I got here. Quickly I correct myself. "Yes, ma'am."

She indicates a chair for me to use but I refuse it. "I prefer to stand, thanks. I am used to operating this while standing on my feet."

I can hear Rockwell muttering to himself as he paces back and forth.

"Okay," says Hughes, "We have our confirmed data link to the drone, and it seems to be in working order!"

I take a couple of deep breaths to steady myself. Well, here goes nothing. "I'm taking her down."

As the drone starts its decent, various people in the room offer their advice.

"You have to remember that there will be a few seconds delay between your reaction time and Venom's response time, so you must take that into consideration when responding to anything."

"The drone will be sensitive to wind turbulence, especially when it is close to the ground so keep a tight rein on it."

"You will have a more limited view than what the camera is actually seeing."

I was about to say that I am used to that, since the only thing that I have flown has been computer generated, but I hold back. I realize that by giving me their tips and advice, these people are accepting me and are only trying to help. I don't want them to think that I am being arrogant or "too big for my britches," as my dad would say. I need to take everything they have to offer me and apply it without question. After all, they are the experts and I am just the middle man they have to use to get their job done.

"Mentally put yourself in that plane, be one with it."

Well I wasn't expecting that. Without even looking, I know that comment came from Captain Rockwell. That is good. I want and need him on my side.

Man, this drone is faster than I expected it to be, but luckily it's responding well to the controller. I spend a minute getting the feel of it and testing to see how sensitive the drone is to the movement of my arm and hand. Every little flex of my muscles, tendons, fingers, and hand has an effect on the stability of the plane so I have to relax my arm and make only slight movements.

Now that I feel like I have good control over Venom I take it down to a lower altitude.

"SAM!" Pigtails yells.

A missile? Already? "Where is it?" I almost scream.

"Coming up fast on your starboard side; right side," she replies.

I don't have time to think, I just automatically respond like it is any other game.

"Wow! Did you see that?" exclaims one of the men. "He turned the plane into the path of the missile and managed to dodge it and then he ducked down behind that ridge. He's too low for the SAMs now. Nice flying, kid."

I feel a surge of adrenaline flow through me. It sounds like they are beginning to gain some confidence in my ability to pull this off. But I still haven't heard my dad say anything.

Suddenly Venom is under fire. Tracers; a lot of them. If every third or fifth round is a tracer, then that means hundreds of bullets are being fired at me, so that means there must be enemy machineguns in the area and they have spotted me. I have to take it down even lower.

I am beginning to think of myself and the drone as being one. Everything happening to Venom I now consider as happening to me. Everyone was right, my vision is limited, but if I am one with the plane, as

Rockwell said, I will be able to fly by instinct and my senses will help to guide me.

"Holy heck! He is flying so low they can't even get a clear shot at him with their machinegun. He is even coming in below the tracers." Whoever it was that said that, sure sounded impressed.

"This drone is incredible," I exclaim excitedly. "It seems to know what I'm going to do before I even do it. It's as if it is a part of me."

"That's the beauty of this model," says Lieutenant Hughes. "It practically flies itself. Although whoever is piloting it commands it to go right, left, up, or down, the drone makes all the intricate corrections pertaining to those movements. Such as the positioning of the flaps, ailerons, rudder, or anything else it needs to adjust in order to make a smooth transition from one movement to the next.

"Only in this case," he continues, "I think the glove and this site's computer are working together to somehow enhance the drone's performance. I haven't figured out exactly how yet though."

"Okay, Stuart," says Pigtails, "just hop that next ridge there, take it up the valley and you should have us lined up for a clean shot."

It is clear to me that she intends to fire the missile herself, probably from the control panel. My only job is to fly the aircraft.

I am passing over the ridge at such a low level that it almost looks like I'm gliding directly over the ground. Up and down over the rough terrain, hugging the ground without touching it. As long as I stay low, even if they can hear me coming, the bad guys won't be able to see me.

This is like the Ploesti raid in World War II. In order to achieve surprise, American B-24 four-engine bombers flew into Romania at tree top level to bomb the oil refineries at Ploesti. It was said that cornstalks were found in the bomb bay doors after the raid. If those pilots could do that with those heavy airplanes, there is no excuse for me to fail here and now, considering the more advanced technological marvels that I have to work with.

I just need to fly up this valley until I can see the target in the mouth of the cave. Easy now; keep it steady. I'm so focused on what I am doing, I'm no longer even nervous.

"There, it is, I can see it!" I can't believe I have done it. I'm almost there.

"Watch it kid!" warns the sergeant major.

"I see them," I yell. But it is seconds too late. There isn't anything I can do about it now. There up ahead of me are a couple of enemy soldiers scrambling to set up their machinegun. There is nothing I can do but stay my course and fly right over them.

Without thinking, I automatically make a downward motion with my thumb, pushing the imaginary button that would fire a missile if I were playing a game. To everyone's shock, the glove and its computer processes that movement, sending a command to the real drone and Venom's missile is launched in a flash.

"What are you doing?" screams Rockwell. "He just fired our only working missile. Now we have no firepower left!"

No one was more surprised than I was when that missile actually launched. It was a reflexive motion on my part that shouldn't have caused anything to happen, but I guess the glove and the computer understood it to mean, "fire!"

The missile flies past the machinegun and its crew and explodes in a ball of fire and smoke. Even though it missed the enemy, it must have scared the heck out of them, because they never even got a shot off at me. Everyone was so busy ducking for cover I was able to fly past them unmolested.

There is the cave dead ahead! I am still heading right for it but what good does it do me now without any more missiles? I am lined up for a perfect shot but am left with nothing to shoot.

The room is dead silent. There is nothing anyone can do except watch to see how this will play out. The air is thick with tension. It is solely up to me and I can only see one thing to do.

Uh oh. The gun crew in the cave has spotted me and is traversing their gun to try and shoot me down, but they are too late.

I am heading straight for them and everyone here in the control room and in that cave have now come to realize what I am about to do. I'm so close that I can see the look of fear and panic on the faces of the gun crew right before they scatter and dive for cover. It is at this second that Pigtails reaches over and slams her palm down on that red self-destruct button.

Bam! All in the room is dead silent as every single person stares intently at the laptop screen even though there is nothing to see now but static. I'm afraid to even breathe. Now that it is over with, I wonder what I have managed to do. Have I messed everything up beyond repair? My hands are starting to shake and it is spreading throughout my whole body. Oh my gosh, what have I done?

Finally the silence is broken by the excited voice of a tech wearing a Cubs cap and head phones. "Colonel, transmission indicates the chopper is on the move. The helicopter is airborne!"

The cheering in the small communications room is deafening. Man, what a relief. I feel like I just made the winning touchdown at the big game. If only Becki was here to see it all. At least my dad did, and he is beaming from ear to ear!

The Cubs fan hits a switch and the room fills with music. He cranks up the volume, slaps on an Iron Man mask, and starts doing the robot dance with another tech who is now Spiderman. Pigtails jumps up and starts dancing wildly. She bounces over and grabs me, swinging me around, and hugging me yelling, "Woohoo, you did it!" I can't help laughing and getting into the spirit of the whole thing even though I can't dance and I know I look ridiculous.

As I pass by him, Captain Rockwell reaches out and claps his Cavalry hat on my head. "Way to go, kid," he calls out. Dad and the sergeant major are just standing on the sidelines savoring the victory in their own way. And this is a great victory!

When things start to calm down I look around the room for my dad but he is no longer here. Why isn't he celebrating and congratulating me like everyone else? My heart sinks and I can't help but to feel disappointed.

Then I look toward the doorway and in he comes, followed by Becki's dad. Before I have time to wonder what in the world he is doing here, I see Becki walk in behind them. They make their way over to me and Mr. Everest shakes my hand while Becki stands shyly to the side. "So young man, I hear congratulations are in order. That was quite an amazing feat you managed to pull off."

"Thank you, sir," I say uncertainly. I still don't know why he is here or how he knows about any of this.

I look to my dad for an explanation and I can see how pleased he is. "You are probably wondering why Mr. Everest is here. I just found out that he is the owner of CyberDan.com and the creator of the gaming glove prototype."

I couldn't have been more surprised if he had suddenly sprouted wings and flew around the room. I turn my attention back to Becki's dad.

"That's right, Stuart. I have been working on it ever since I lost my job and I have been running the game competition out of the coffee shop downtown. That is where Becki found me this morning after you were so unceremoniously removed from the school bus. She was worried about you and she wanted me to find out if you were okay."

I glance at Becki and we exchange a smile. She was worried about me? That must mean she cares. I can't believe it.

"It just so happened that I was monitoring my site when the request to relinquish control to the government came in. Once I figured out what was happening and where the request had originated from, we rushed over here to see if there was anything I could do to assist."

"Unfortunately," Dad puts in, "he was not allowed through the gate because of the high level of security involved.

"Now if you will excuse us, I would like to introduce Mr. Everest to everyone." With that they walk away leaving me and Becki alone. "Thank you, Becki," I tell her.

"Oh I didn't do anything, Stuart. You're the one who saved the day. Your dad told us everything you did. Why, you are a hero!"

Me, a hero? Wow, that thought never occurred to me. "I'm glad you're here, Becki. There is no one else I would rather share this with."

"I'm glad I'm here too," she responds shyly.

"Becki, I have to know; there was a fairy named Moonbeam in one of my games. I've been dying to know if that was you."

She looks at me with an impish grin and says, "I can tell you now but I couldn't before. Yes, I was Moonbeam. I knew that Mandor was you because my dad told me, but I wasn't allowed to talk to anyone about the games and what he was doing."

Becki smiles and takes my hand in hers. "There is nowhere else I would rather be right now, Mandor."

Bursting with pride, I hold onto her hand and I never want to let go. Yes, I am proud of what I have done, but I think I am even prouder that Becki is standing at my side, holding my hand.

On the ride home Dad and I finally get a chance to talk. "Son, I have always been proud of you, but today you have earned a new respect from me. There were times when I thought you were wasting your time and talents on those video games, but now I think maybe I should have you show me a thing or two about them. Even though I didn't agree with all of the time you put into them, I still followed your progress in that computer game competition because I knew it was important to you.

"As a matter of fact I have even been thinking of taking pottery classes with your mom, because that is something that is important to her. That way we can spend some time together doing something that *she* enjoys."

"Uh, Dad, I wouldn't say that in front of your army buddies or you just might get another codename that you don't like as much as Buttercup."

I can't believe it. I actually got him to smile!

Chapter Twenty

Thankfully, everyone survived that day and there was no need for my dad to relay any deathbed messages to loved ones. Needless to say, even though the mission was a success, and I am a hero, we aren't allowed to talk about it. It is so top secret that I can't even tell Mark, and Dad had a serious discussion with Martin Everest and Becki, stressing the importance of their silence.

Of course my Dad, in his line of work, knows how to keep secrets himself. And my mom, being married to him for so many years, knows that there will always be secrets that have to be kept. There are many times when he has worked late, received mysterious phone calls in the middle of the night, or had to go out of town for extended periods of time, but she knows that it is work related and even if she asked, he couldn't share it with her. But she understands the grave danger he is in at times, and her concern is not for what he is doing, but for whether he will survive to come back to her at all. She has seen enough closed caskets over the years to know just what a dangerous profession he has chosen for himself.

And after what we had been through together that morning, I learned to open up and talk to my dad. So, I told him everything. I told him about how Mark had brought his toy gun to school in order to scare Todd, which led to my telling him the circumstances behind my skipping school that day. And I told him about Todd and his brother Derik and how they made life miserable for kids like me. I told him about the homeless guy in the tunnel and how I had been afraid at first but then I had helped him out by giving him Mark's lunch and our money. And while I was spilling my guts, I told him about my concerns about Mom looking so sad and Dad seeming angry lately. I even worked up the nerve to ask him outright, whether they might have been fighting, and were they perhaps thinking about getting a divorce. My biggest fear, which I kept to myself and didn't tell him, was that the trouble between them was my fault and that they were fighting over problems that I had caused.

To my extreme relief, he told me that they were definitely not getting a divorce and that they weren't really even fighting at all. It turns out that the rude guy in the black SUV outside of the tailor shop has been harassing my mother ever since that incident. Whenever he saw her on the road, he would follow her trying to cut her off and he would yell insults at her. The last straw was when she became so upset when he was behind her in a parking lot honking and yelling that she stepped on the brake pedal too sharply and he actually ran into the back of her car. He became so angry that he jumped out of his vehicle and was screaming at her blaming her for the accident and when she wouldn't get out of her car, he kicked the driver door so hard he put a dent in it.

My dad was furious, and wanted to track him down to deal with him in his own way, which would probably be the same way that he would have dealt with a terrorist in Iraq. But my mom wanted to let the police handle it, even though the other driver ended up outright lying about it all. So Mom and Dad's disagreements had stemmed from them not being able to agree on how to handle the whole situation. I don't blame my dad for overreacting. It made me angry too, to think that someone was being so mean and upsetting my mom.

———————

It is funny how some things seemed so hopeless at the time but now months later everything is completely different. I must admit that me finally trusting in my dad and opening up to him played a big part in why things have improved in my life.

It turns out that my dad had a hand in the training of State Police drone pilots for their prototype "eye in the sky." This was a fairly new program that worked hand in hand with surveillance cameras at the major intersections. It was designed to monitor traffic on the roads for unsafe drivers, and in particular, those who have been charged and found guilty of previous traffic offenses got special attention. One of those vehicles that received special attention was a certain black SUV with dark tinted windows which was caught on tape several times driving recklessly around a little, red car.

I was shocked, but then again it all made perfect sense, when I found out that the driver was none other than Todd and Derik's father. I guess bullying runs in their family and the kids were just following the example set by their parent. He was found guilty of hitting my mom's car, harassment, and threatening her with bodily harm. He had to pay for the damage and he received a year of community service. Since he will lose his driver's license for one more offense, he is a much less aggressive driver now. At least now I know my mom will be safe on the road.

And then there is Becki's dad, Mr. Everest. There he was, out of work with no home, and with a family to take care of. Luckily the family pulled together during their time of hardship instead of falling apart. Mr. Everest's development of the gaming glove ended up saving their family. With the help of my dad, many doors were opened and Mr. Everest has won a major military defense contract for his glove. They plan on using a lot of drones in the future, and what better way to control them than with a state of the art precision glove controller? Thankfully, Becki's days of living in a tent are behind her and she has a normal home life once again.

Dad even went so far as to track down Sal the homeless veteran and set him up with a job working for Mr. Everest. It turns out that Sal's military training included computer repair and all he needed was a lucky break to prove that he was good at it. With his war injury, he isn't able to work long hours at a time but Mr. Everest understood about that and he set Sal up with a computer so he can work from home. And yes, he too has a home now, thanks to my dad.

My dad has worked hard to fix things for me. That is what a good parent strives to do for their children. It took me a long time to see that he is a good parent and he was never against me. He was on my side all along.

Fixing something means different things to different people. To a young child, it could mean a broken toy has been repaired. To an adolescent, it may be working to mend a fractured friendship. To an adult, it might entail saying you are sorry even though it was not your fault. By the simplest definition, to fix something is to mend, repair, or restore it.

Many other things have been mended, repaired, and restored too. Take Kim's problem for instance. An allergy to peanuts was discovered and now her face has cleared up completely. She is not as vain as she used to be now that she realizes you can't rely solely on a pretty face to get you through life. Thanks to Humphrey's help, she works harder at her schoolwork and she makes it a point to be friendly towards everyone, not just the popular kids. But her very best friend out of everyone is the guy who saw her as beautiful when others could not, so no one dares say a bad word about Humphrey when she is around.

As for Toni, Kim's cyber-bully, I heard that she lost her cell phone and the person that found it took her pictures and videos and posted them on the internet. The pictures showed her at parties, drinking and doing drugs and the video was of her complaining about having to work with handicapped kids to get her achievement award. She was calling the unfortunate kids bad names and imitating their speech. It turned out that it was one of her so-called friends who posted these images. I guess it's like my mom always says, what goes around comes around. Unfortunately, Toni's parents haven't followed through with punishing her on their end. Even though she was kicked off of the cheer squad, they are fighting to get her back on. No matter what she does wrong, her parents still spoil her and give her anything she wants or demands. No wonder the girl has problems.

And then there is Todd. I can't tell you if this is true or not but I heard a rumor that he was on the beach one Saturday afternoon tossing a football with some friends when a group of young, muscular men dressed in camouflage came jogging by in the surf. The men suddenly all veered off and surrounded Todd. Like I said, I can't say for sure that this is true but Todd's buddies talked about it for days afterward. They laughed about how scared Todd was to find himself in the middle of a group of soldiers sporting tattoos such as "Death from Above" and "Air Cav." I have no idea what they said to him but after that his friends realized he wasn't as tough as he made himself out to be and they stopped looking up to him. I wish I could say that Todd was a changed man after that incident but not everything in life is that simple. Derik and his friends still look up to him so Todd just hangs around with those younger kids now. I have to admit that whenever Todd starts picking on me again, I purposely wear one of my "Airborne Rangers" t-shirts to school to help remind him that it might be healthier for him to turn his attention elsewhere.

As far as my friendship with Mark goes, it is as strong as it ever was. We make a good team and we will always have each other's backs. Besides, without me, who would keep him out of trouble?

Last but certainly not least, is my relationship with Becki. She is my girlfriend now and I'm as proud as I can be about that! Next year I will get my driver's license, and when I do my dad has told me the Mustang will be mine. I can hardly wait to drive Becki to school. I imagine us riding together with the music cranked up and the windows down and the wind blowing through her hair. From my rear view mirror I will hang her necklace, the silver quarter-moon. That way, whenever I am driving, all I will have to do is see it dangling there and I will know that she is always with me, my beautiful Fairy Princess of Matterhorn.